My Dad's *Definitely* Not a Drunk!

Elisa Lynn Carbone

WATERFRONT BOOKS
Burlington, Vermont 05401

Edited by Susan B. Weber
Cover illustration by Hendrik Glaeser
Typography by Bold Face Graphics

Printed in the United States

LCCN: 92-053883

ISBN: 0-914525-21-2 cloth
0-914525-22-0 paper

Distributed to the trade by
The Talman Company
131 Spring Street, Suite 201 E-N
New York, NY 10012
1-800-537-8894

For Jim
and
for Nina

Chapter 1

It wasn't Corey's first time on the school roof, but it was her first time up there with Alexandra, David, and a bag of water balloons. She reached down to grab Alex's hand and help her from a wobbly branch of the oak tree onto the roof. The flat tarred and gravelled surface shimmered in the afternoon sun.

"It's hot up here," Corey complained.

"It wasn't my idea. Blame it on David," said Alex. She ran both hands through her tight brown curls.

Corey lifted her own hair off her neck and wiped the sweat from her cheeks. She looked down at the three backpacks that lay in the grass at the base of the oak: David's khaki, Alex's dirty yellow, and her own hot pink. Looking down made her dizzy.

David was already on his stomach at the front edge of the roof, the bag of water balloons at his side. He motioned to Corey and Alex and they crept toward him on hands and knees. Mr. Gavin, one of the fifth grade teachers, walked out the school's front doors.

"Hold your fire!" David ordered.

Alex rolled her eyes. "He thinks he's in the marines already," she whispered to Corey.

Corey pulled a floppy water balloon out of the bag

1

and tossed it lightly from one hand to another. "So we just throw them down and duck, and we don't get in trouble?" she asked.

"Shhh. Someone's coming," said David.

Alex held a balloon by its knotted end. "Fire?" she asked.

David shook his head. His dark eyes shifted from Alex to Corey. "Wait for the Grim-Man," he answered.

"David, you're nuts!" Alex punched him in the arm. "You want to get us all expelled? Or killed by Dr. Grimwater?"

"Yeah," agreed Corey. "Throwing water balloons at the principal isn't too bright. It'll get us at least two weeks detention."

"They can't give us two weeks detention," said David. "There's only one week of school left." He held a green balloon up and swung it gently. "And they can't really expel us either, since we're all going to junior high next year."

Suddenly the heavy metal doors creaked open again. Corey saw Dr. Grimwater's pale, bald head rimmed with red hair. She heard David mutter, "Fire!" and felt the soft water balloon fly from her hand.

They trotted across the roof, crouched over and giggling. The rough bark of the oak tree scraped Corey's hands as she swung from branch to branch to the ground. Then the three of them ran, laughing and gasping, all the way to Corey's house.

"Made it!" declared Corey as she flopped down on the shaded porch steps.

"Mission accomplished," said David, grinning. He noticed the ancient Oldsmobile parked in front of Corey's house. "Is your mom home from work early or something?" he asked.

"No," said Corey. "She takes the Metro in sometimes because that old car breaks down a lot." She pulled her house keys out of her shorts pocket and let the sweaty group into the house. Yofi, her golden retriever, nearly knocked her over with his enthusiastic greeting.

"You're lucky that your mom works," said Alex. "It must be nice to have the house to yourself after school."

"What's the matter, Alex, don't you like your mom?" teased David.

Alex shot him a glare that could kill.

"What did I say?" David was surprised.

Corey shook her head briefly at Alex with a "don't worry about it — he doesn't know" look. Out loud she said, "Let's get something to drink," and led them into the kitchen.

"What's on tap?" asked David. He plopped onto a stool at the breakfast bar.

"Iced tea, apple juice, and seltzer water," answered Corey.

"I'll have a beer," said David.

"I'll take a vodka and tonic," said Alex.

"Coming right up," said Corey. She poured three glasses of iced tea.

"Whatter you drinkin', Cor?" asked David, with a drunken slurr.

"Um . . . a martini." She flicked her straight blonde hair back over her shoulders with the kind of grace she imagined women used in bars.

"What's going on in there?" a voice called from the den.

Corey froze. "Mom?" she squeaked.

A thin, pretty woman with worried eyes walked into the kitchen. She carried an armload of boxes.

"We were just pretending, Mom. We're really drinking iced tea. See?"

"Hi, David. Hi, Alex," said Mrs. O'Dell, the worried look still there. "Could you three please help me carry some more of this inventory up from the basement?"

"Sure," they answered.

The O'Dells' basement looked like a warehouse for lost knicknacks. Boxes with labels like: Posters (Monuments/Cherry Blossoms); White House T-Shirts; Ashtrays/Hats/Pencils (Capitol) lined the walls.

Mrs. O'Dell loaded their arms with as many boxes as they could carry.

"What's all this stuff?" asked David.

"The usual Washington, D.C. souvenirs. When people visit the nation's capital they like to have something to show for it."

"Why are we bringing up so much today?" asked Corey.

Her mother turned and began to rearrange a row of boxes on a shelf. "It's going to be a busy weekend," she answered.

"You're going to work all weekend again?" Corey's

voice rose. She dropped her boxes onto the basement floor and stood with her arms crossed.

Alex and David hurried up the steps and out of sight with their cartons.

"Corey," said her mother, "I don't want to work all weekend any more than you want me to, but we need the money."

"What about Daddy?" interrupted Corey, "Why doesn't he work on the weekends instead of you? And why can't he get a good job like he used to have instead of that stupid salesman job."

"Cora-Ann O'Dell, I don't ever want to hear you call your father 'stupid' again!"

"I didn't call him stupid!" Corey was close to tears, and she was sorry she'd mentioned her father at all.

Her mother sat down on a box. "I'm sorry," she said quietly, "I guess I'm just tired and cranky these days."

She looked up, her eyes brighter. "How would you like to help me at the store this weekend?"

Corey managed a smile. "That would be great," she said. "I've been practicing my sales routine, too. Listen to this: Hello there, may I help you? Yes, of course, we have genuine Washington, D.C. toilet paper holders. Would you like the Jefferson Memorial model or the Smithsonian model?"

Her mom laughed. "Okay, Miss Personality. Now go do your weekend homework so you won't be worrying about it on Sunday night."

"I've just got two math papers to finish. They're in my backpa–."

An unfriendly chill crept up Corey's spine. She edged toward the steps. "I'll go get them," she said, then whirled and dashed to the kitchen, where Alex and David were playing with Yofi.

"Our backpacks!" she whispered between clenched teeth. She didn't need to say more. David led the way out the door, down the street, and across the playing fields to the school. They dashed around the corner of the building. There stood the oak tree, its leaves shifting slightly in the breeze. The backpacks were gone.

"Great," groaned Alex. "If my backpack's stolen, my dad is going to make me pay for it."

"Who would want your grubby old backpack?" said David. "Monday morning, we're going to wish they were stolen. Old Grimwater must have come here to find out who hit him with the water balloons. We were too fast for him, but too dumb to pick up our packs."

"And now he knows who did it," said Corey. They sat down hard on the grass.

"I hate getting in trouble," said Alex.

"Me, too," said David.

Corey smiled sheepishly. "I didn't finish my lunch, and it's still in my pack," she said. "It's going to be really disgusting by Monday morning."

"Gross," said Alex. "I hope he locked the packs in his office for the weekend. When he calls us in, we'll say, 'Uh, excuse me, Dr. Grimwater, but I think you might need some air freshener in here.' "

They laughed. Somehow, with only five days of school left, even facing a furious Dr. Grimwater didn't seem so bad.

Chapter 2

Saturday morning Corey took a sleepy-eyed look at her digital clock. It was 7:32 and already there was water running in her parents' bathroom. She rolled over and tried to go back to sleep.

"Wake up, kiddo!" Her father came into the room and raised the blinds. "Mom's leaving for the shop in an hour."

"I'm getting up." She yawned, closed her eyes, and snuggled deeper under the covers.

"Come on, big girl." He grabbed a foot that stuck out of the covers and tickled it.

"Okay, okay," Corey giggled and sat up. "I'm awake."

She blinked at her father. He looked out of place so early on a Saturday morning. "What are you doing up?" she asked. She tried to hide the "It's about time you got up before noon" in her voice.

"New job," he said briskly. "I'm working for Burt's Lawn Service, and the grass and flowers get up good and early, even on Saturdays." He slipped out her bedroom door toward the smell of coffee wafting up from the kitchen.

So he'd lost another job. Corey rubbed her eyes and squinted out the window at two squirrels running across the back fence. No sense letting the bad news wreck her morning. The good news was that he was up and in a good mood, and if she got dressed quickly they could have breakfast together.

She pulled on a T-shirt and shorts, and styled her bangs with a curling iron until they looked just right. Then she raced down the steps and collided with her father, who was on his way up.

"I was just coming to ask what you want for breakfast," he said. "I'm cooking, and you can't stop me." Over his jeans he wore a red apron with white lace around the edges.

"Nice outfit," said Corey. "How about scrambled eggs and toast and strawberries?"

"Sounds terrific. You want the strawberries on the toast or in the scrambled eggs?" he asked.

"Daddy, you're silly." She laughed.

When her father was in a good mood, Corey felt like he was the best dad in the whole world. He could still pick her up and swing her around even though she was "growing up way too fast," as he put it. And when he hugged her, his clean shirts smelled like soap and sunshine.

"What time will you ladies be home?" he asked as he sliced strawberries into a bowl.

Corey liked being referred to as a lady.

"I'll close the shop at six," Mom replied. "We're taking the car to cart all that inventory, so we should be home by seven if that old clunker keeps moving."

"You shouldn't talk about the Oldsmobile like that,"

Dad teased. "It might take offense and break down on purpose."

Corey ate her breakfast listening to her parents talk. Their conversation was light and easy on this sunny morning. Yofi laid his head on her lap to beg, so she gave him her toast crusts and scratched him behind the ears. Yofi never could seem to get enough food or attention.

The Oldsmobile sputtered its way around the beltway, heading toward the Connecticut Avenue exit that would take them into the city to Dupont Circle.

"Corey, do you know the Donatellis?" Mom asked. "They moved into the new townhouses. The boy's name is Victor. I think he's in the eighth grade."

At the mention of Victor's name, Corey's stomach did a little flip. Sure, she thought, I know where he lives, I know the color of his eyes, and that he wears an I.D. bracelet with his initials engraved on it.

"They just leased a storefront on P street near our shop," Corey's mother continued cheerily. "They're opening a bakery. Last weekend they moved their equipment in and Victor was there helping them, so you might see him there this week, too."

Corey gripped the door handle as if it were the safety bar on a roller coaster. Having a mad crush on Victor from afar was manageable. But she definitely could not face him. Then a terrifying thought struck her. What if he came into the shop to buy something?

Corey's heart pounded, and she felt her face turn red just thinking about it.

"Corey, are you all right? Are you getting carsick?"

"I'm okay, Mom," Corey said weakly. "It's just . . . uh, I'll open the window." She rolled down the window and inhaled a blast of diesel exhaust from a bus. She pretended to feel much better.

Her mother began to circle, looking for a parking space. "Look," she said, "they've got their sign up already, Donatelli's Bread and Pastry Shop."

Corey slid down low in her seat. Through the plate glass windows of the bakery she saw two people who must be Mr. and Mrs. Donatelli, but not Victor. She breathed a sigh of relief and scooted back up in her seat.

"Corey, what in the world are you doing?" her mother asked.

"Um . . . my back itches. I'm scratching it against the car seat."

"A parking space!" exclaimed her mom. The chances of finding a parking space at Dupont Circle were only a little better than those of winning the Maryland lottery. "We'll park here now and open the shop. Once we get the storage room organized we can bring all the boxes in."

When they got to the shop they found a family of four looking in the windows.

"Mighty glad you showed up with the key, ma'am," said the man. His huge belly stuck out of his Washington, D.C. T-shirt and hung over his jeans. "Me and the

10

wife and kids here are headed back home this mornin'. Like to do some last-minute shopping before we leave."

Mrs. O'Dell unlocked the door and invited them in. The two boys, both skinny and blonde, rummaged through the monument photographs and postcards. The woman, who was as round and soft as her husband, delicately handled a porcelain statue of Abraham Lincoln.

Mrs. O'Dell chatted politely with the husband and wife, answering their questions. She told them how her parents had bought the shop back in 1952 and left it to her when they retired.

They picked out two small statues, one of President Thomas Jefferson and one of President Lincoln, and each boy bought a baseball cap with a picture of the Capitol and "The Nation's Capitol" printed on the front.

All morning customers came and went. By noon they'd met people from Louisiana, Minnesota, Quebec, and Germany and had sold $226.97 worth of gifts and souvenirs. They'd also had time to prepare the storage room for the new inventory. Corey's mother moved the car to the unloading zone in front of the store, and after they had carried all the boxes inside, left to find a new parking place.

Two women in business suits came into the store. Corey squared her shoulders. "May I help you?" she asked.

"No, thanks," said one. "Just looking," said the other. They left without buying anything.

11

Corey decided the display shelves needed cleaning. As she reached under the counter to get the Windex and paper towels, the bells on the front door jingled. When she looked up, she nearly fell over. Victor Donatelli had just walked into the shop.

Corey opened her mouth to say "Hi," but nothing came out. Victor looked at her and smiled. Corey closed her mouth.

"Hi," he said.

Corey's palms began to sweat. She wished she'd brushed her teeth after lunch.

"Hi," she whispered, then ducked down behind the counter. Mom, she thought, please find a parking space and come back quickly! She hugged the roll of paper towels, wondering how long she could stay there before Victor noticed something was wrong.

"Watcha doin'?" came Victor's voice from directly above her head. He leaned over the countertop and peered down at her.

Corey held out the paper towels. "Cleaning up," she squeaked.

"Well, if you're busy, I won't bother you. I was wondering if you could help me pick out something for my mom. It's her birthday next week."

Corey stood up and brushed herself off. Here she was, alone with Victor Donatelli, actually talking to him. Well, sort of talking to him.

At that moment, her mother breezed in the door. "I tell you, this is my lucky day for parking spaces. Oh, hi, Victor. How are things at the bakery?"

"Everything is fine, Mrs. O'Dell. We opened for business this morning."

"Well, if Corey gets bored later, maybe I'll ask her to pick up some cookies."

Victor nodded and smiled at Corey. "I'd better get back now. It's been really busy today."

Corey fled to the bathroom. She splashed cold water on her face, then took a look in the mirror.

"Why do you have to be so nervous?" she asked the face in the mirror. "Why can't you just act normal and hold a regular conversation with somebody?"

Because Victor Donatelli comes from a regular, normal family—and you don't, answered her reflection. He belongs. You don't.

She slumped back against the wall and closed her eyes.

Daddy was okay this morning, she thought. He was up and dressed and happy. He made me breakfast and went to work. She sighed, wiped the water from her cheeks, and walked slowly back to the counter.

"Isn't Victor a nice boy? And so handsome, too," her mother rambled on as she rearranged some postcards. "And it's nice to have someone your age around here, don't you think?"

"He's not my age," said Corey flatly. "He's two grades older than I am."

Their conversation was interrupted by a customer who wanted to buy souvenir place mats.

The afternoon passed quickly. Corey told her mother she'd been inspired by their dental hygienist to give up sweets and didn't think cookies from the bakery were a good idea.

During the ride home, Corey rested her head against the seat and closed her eyes. She replayed the scene with Victor over and over in her mind, imagining the things she wished she'd said, trying to blot out the memory of what a klutz she'd been.

As they pulled up to the house, Corey's father was standing in the front yard, still dressed in the red apron, talking to the next-door neighbors. His voice was loud and he gestured widely with one hand as he talked. When Corey saw what was in his other hand, her stomach knotted.

He held a small, green bottle, lifted it to his lips, and took a long drink.

Corey got out of the car and walked quickly toward the house, her eyes down.

"Hey, how's my big working girl?" her father called.

Corey stopped. His words were clear, not slurred.

"I was just telling Mr. and Mrs. Saunders here how they could landscape their whole front yard," he said. "Make it look like a million dollars."

He held out one arm for a hug and Corey walked cautiously to him. She glanced at the bottle in his hand. It was only a soda. The knot in her stomach loosened.

"So, how was your day at the shop?" he asked her. "Are you hungry?"

"I'm starved," she answered. She smiled politely at Mr. and Mrs. Saunders.

"Good. Because that delicious aroma you might have noticed is coming from our backyard."

Corey sniffed. Burgers!

They sat around the patio table as the sunlight faded and the lightning bugs and mosquitoes came out. Finally, Corey decided she'd had enough to eat, and that the mosquitoes had eaten enough of her, so she went inside.

Her mother's voice drifted in through the screen door, "I'm happy, Steven. Really, I'm so glad...."

"Don't act so surprised," said her father, "I told you I was turning over a new leaf. Everything is going to be different from now on."

After that, everything grew quiet. Corey figured they were kissing, so she went upstairs and got ready for bed.

Chapter 3

Corey sat at her desk and chewed on a pencil. Three hundred and fifteen kids. Two sixth grades. Mrs. Higgins and a whole bunch of other teachers. And now, over the intercom, they were all going to hear her name announced.

"Please return all library books before the last day of school," the voice over the intercom droned. "Be sure all lunch money accounts are paid." Oh, just go ahead and say it, thought Corey.

"Alexandra Williams, David Liederman, and Cora-Ann O'Dell, please report to Dr. Grimwater's office immediately. This concludes the morning announcements."

Every kid in the room stared at Corey. Mrs. Higgins raised her eyebrows. "Corey, I hope this isn't anything serious," she said.

What, exactly, would be something "serious"? Corey wondered. Blowing up the school, that's serious. Murder, armed robbery, spray painting the cafeteria walls — very serious. No, this was not serious.

Corey shook her head. "I probably just have an overdue library book or something." She slipped out the door before Mrs. Higgins could ask more questions.

Outside the office, Alex stood waiting for her.

"Where's David?" Corey asked.

"He stopped in the boys' room. Said he has some kind of plan to keep us out of trouble."

"What kind of a plan?"

"I don't know. He won't tell me a thing. Oh, good, here he comes."

David walked down the hall, grinning. "Hello, Cora-Ann. Hello, Alexandra," he teased.

"Cut it out, David," said Alex.

"Yeah," agreed Corey, "and what's this plan you've got?"

"You'll see," he answered.

David opened the office door and the three of them walked inside. Mrs. Dorsel, the secretary, peered at them over the top of her glasses like a bug-eyed ostrich.

"May I help you children?" she asked in her usual distracted way.

"We're supposed to see Dr. Grimwater," said Alex.

"Oh, yes, of course." She narrowed her eyes at them disapprovingly. "Go right in. He's expecting you."

As Corey walked past the desk, she could feel Mrs. Dorsel's eyes follow her.

The principal's office smelled faintly of rotten tuna and sour milk. Dr. Grimwater was at his desk, bent studiously over a pile of papers. Corey studied the freckles on the top of his bald head.

They stood in a line with David in the middle and waited. Then, without looking up, Dr. Grimwater asked in a syrupy-sweet voice, "So, did you children manage to get your homework done over the week-end?"

David poked Corey in the side with his elbow.

"Uh, no, sir," answered Corey, "I didn't get mine done."

Dr. Grimwater finally looked at her. "Oh? And why was that, young lady?"

Corey wondered why, with all three of them there, she was the only one answering questions.

"Because I didn't have my backpack with all my papers in it, sir," she answered.

Dr. Grimwater rose and began to pace back and forth across the room like a lawyer questioning a witness.

"And can you tell me why you didn't have your backpack with all your papers in it?" he asked, the sweetness quickly draining from his voice.

Corey elbowed David, but he just elbowed her back. She reached around behind him and jabbed Alex in the ribs with two fingers. Alex coughed and started talking,

"Well, uh, you see . . . Sir, you want to know why we didn't have our backpacks?"

Dr. Grimwater turned on his heel, his eyes wide with fake surprise. "Oh my!" he exclaimed. "Do you mean to tell me that you didn't have *your* backpack either, Miss Williams? What a strange coincidence! And what about you, Mr. Liederman? Did something mysterious happen to your backpack as well?" By now Dr. Grimwater's voice was downright nasty.

David stood there with a terrified look on his face. Then all of a sudden he doubled over, gagged, and threw up all over the floor.

Dr. Grimwater gasped and jumped back like an hysterical monkey. "Mrs. Dorsel," he shouted. "Call the nurse! Call the janitor! Get these children out of here!"

He snatched the backpacks off the floor and shoved them at Corey and Alex. "Take these smelly things away and don't let me ever catch you anywhere near that roof again!"

Mrs. Dorsel herded them quickly out of the office. Dr. Grimwater fled down the hall toward the teachers' lounge, his handkerchief clasped over his mouth and nose.

Out in the hall, David burst out laughing. Corey looked at him as if he'd gone absolutely crazy.

"Come on, David," she said. "We'd better get you to the nurse. You might have a stomach virus or something."

David was laughing so hard he couldn't talk.

"Cool it, David," said Alex. "Are you sick, or were you just scared to pieces, or what?"

David motioned them to the corner near the drinking fountain. He unbuttoned his shirt. Corey watched in awe as he showed them a plastic bag with rubber bands holding it to a plastic tube. The tube opened near the neck of his shirt, and in the bag was what looked like milk with creamed corn, pieces of leaves, and chopped nuts. It smelled terrible. In fact, it looked and smelled exactly like the mess he'd deposited all over Dr. Grimwater's office floor.

"What in the world *is* this stuff?" asked Corey, screwing up her face.

"It's Magic Mess," answered David proudly. "There was a recipe for it in my magic kit. It's guaranteed to look and smell just like real throw-up."

"Jeez, David. You're disgusting!" Alex groaned.

"It kept us out of trouble, didn't it?" he said with a satisfied smile.

Corey realized he was right. No detention, no extra homework, no suspension, no notes home to their parents, no nothing.

"David, you're a genius," said Alex.

"Thank you, Alexandra."

"Shut up, you creep, or I'll think of some obnoxious name to call you."

"Okay, okay," said David. "Well, I'd better wash up and change my clothes, or kids will have lots of terrible names to call me by the end of the day." He headed toward the boys' room.

"I guess I'd better get back to class," said Corey.

"I'm going to wait for David so we both walk in at the same time," said Alex.

"Okay. Hey, I tried to call you over the weekend. I kept getting no answer. Did your family go on a trip or something?"

Alex leaned against the wall, her hands in the pockets

of her shorts. For the first time that morning, Corey noticed how tired she looked.

"No, we didn't go anywhere. Nobody wanted to answer the phone, that's all," said Alex.

"Alex, you shouldn't do that! What if you had an emergency call?"

Alex shrugged.

"You mean your parents just let the phone ring, too?"

"My dad had to work all weekend," Alex answered flatly.

"And your mom—" Corey stopped herself. Suddenly the picture became clear. Alex's tiredness, her grouchy mood; it all made sense. Corey cleared her throat. "Bad weekend, huh?"

Alex breathed out a long sigh. "Yeah. Real bad," she said.

They stood silently for a moment, looking down at the grey-speckled tile floor.

"So, how was *your* weekend?" asked Alex, trying to lift the heaviness from her voice.

"Good," answered Corey. She actually felt apologetic about how nice her weekend had been. "My dad stopped drinking again—but you know how long that lasts." She laughed nervously. She wanted more than anything for it to last forever, but felt guilty being happy when Alex was so miserable.

"Yeah, I know," said Alex with the lively bite back in her voice. "It lasts about two seconds and then it's party time!" She twirled once, then danced sloppily across the hall, an imaginary drink in her hand.

Corey giggled. "Alex, stop! You're going to get us in trouble again!"

David arrived with a clean blue shirt on. He smelled like rest room soap.

"Look at that," he said. "It's Alexandra, the dancing street lady."

"Okay, Dufus Brain, that does it," said Alex. "From now on, your name is Dufus Brain."

"Come on, Alex, can't you take a joke? I'll stop calling you Alexandra now. It's Alex from now on. Okay?"

"Okay, Dufus Brain." She smiled innocently.

"Alex! I hate it when you call me Dufus Brain. My parents didn't name me that. Your parents did name you Alexandra."

His logic was lost on Alex. "Come on, Dufus Brain, let's get back to class." She grabbed his arm and led him away.

Corey headed for her own classroom. She could hear Alex and David arguing all the way down the hall.

Chapter 4

By the first day of summer vacation the air was already as hot and humid as a steam bath, and the pollution index had reached the unhealthy range. Every house in the neighborhood was shut tight and air conditioners hummed noisily. Corey slept that morning until 10:00 A.M., then bumbled down the steps in her long T-shirt and underwear to find something for breakfast. She was ready for a long, lazy summer.

Her mother had already left for the shop, and her father sat at the kitchen table reading the newspaper.

"Mornin', Daddy." Corey yawned. "Aren't you going to work today?"

"This heat wave has bought me a day of rest," he said cheerfully. "Roofers and landscapers are supposed to take the day off so they don't drop dead from heatstroke on the job and inconvenience their employers." He put down his newspaper and leaned toward her. "How about we see if there are any tickets left for the Orioles game today?"

"That would be great! But—" Corey's enthusiasm drained quickly, "that means we'd have to go outside."

"Yes, but we would be having fun outside. That's different from working outside. And we can stop at the pool on the way back."

"Okay," said Corey. The pool part sounded the best, but she was always happy to go somewhere with her father.

"Do you want to invite a friend to go with us?" he asked.

David loved baseball, but he was spending most of the summer at his dad's house in Annapolis. Corey picked up the phone and called Alex. She waited as patiently as she could through ten rings.

"I guess they're not home, huh?" asked her father.

Corey put down the receiver slowly. "Yeah, I guess not," she said.

"Well, don't look so glum," he said. "We can have a good time just the two of us, can't we?"

"Of course we can, Daddy! It's just—I think Alex might be there. She might not have heard the phone. Maybe they're all outside working in the garden."

"In this heat?"

"How about if I ride my bike over there to check?"

"That's fine by me," said her father. "Just be ready to leave for the game by noon."

Corey ate breakfast, then ran upstairs and pulled on her shortest shorts and lightest cotton shirt. When she opened the front door the heat hit her like a fist. The sky glared hazy white, with a layer of brown near the horizon. The front lawn looked fried. Even the birds sounded wilted.

"Maybe we should skip the game and just do the pool," she called to her father.

"Don't be such a wimp!" he called back.

She closed the door behind her. Sweat dribbled down her neck and arms even before she'd gotten her bike out of the garage.

As she pedaled the two miles to Alex's house, Corey remembered the day last fall when she had first made this trip. The day she decided to surprise Alex with her new bike and found the front door wide open. No one answered when she rang the bell. She'd timidly pushed the screen door ajar and peeked into the living room. There was Alex's mother in her nightgown passed out on the couch, drunk.

Corey winced, remembering how angry Alex had been when she came down the foyer steps and caught her staring wide-eyed at her mother.

"Get out of here!" she'd screamed, and she had pushed Corey out the door, yelling that her mother was very sick and needed peace and quiet.

Corey remembered how relieved she'd felt at finding out the truth. And she'd refused to pretend to believe Alex's lies.

"It's okay," she had said. "My father does the same thing."

Since that day, they'd been like partners in crime, sharing the shameful family secret. They didn't talk about it much, but just knowing that someone else understood meant everything to Corey. It was like having the sister she'd always wished for.

As she rode her bike through the heat, she knew she

might well find the same kind of scene at Alex's house today. Only this time Alex wouldn't be angry at her for knowing.

She turned onto Alex's street and whizzed down the sidewalk under a line of shady maple trees. Her brakes squeaked as she slowed to turn into the driveway.

Alex sat on the front porch, her skinny legs sticking out of a pair of yellow shorts. She and her little sister, Laura, were playing Chutes and Ladders.

"Hi," said Corey as she dismounted. "What are you guys doing outside? Is your air-conditioning broken or something?"

"What are *you* doing outside?" Alex shot back.

Corey was sorry she'd asked. Couldn't she have guessed it was a bad weekend when they didn't answer the phone?

"I came to invite you to an Orioles game. Me and my dad are going, and he said I could bring a friend."

Alex flicked the spinner with her forefinger, then moved her player. "I can't. I have to take care of Laura," she said.

Corey sat down on a step and fanned herself with the top of the Chutes and Ladders box.

"Do you wanna play with us, Corey?" asked Laura. She wrapped her arms around Corey's neck and hung on her.

"Laura, stop, you're strangling me," said Corey, gently loosening her grip. Laura smelled like no one had given her a bath for a few days.

"Sorry, I can't play with you. My dad said to be home in time to go to the game."

"I thought your mom didn't let your dad drive you anywhere when he's sauced," said Alex.

"He's not," said Corey.

"He's not driving? Then who is?"

"He's not sauced," she said firmly.

"Alex, who is that out there?" a groggy woman's voice called from inside the house. "Is somebody selling something?"

Alex shot a nervous glance at Corey. She didn't need to say a word for Corey to know it was time to leave.

Corey trotted down the steps and hopped onto her bike. "I'll call you tomorrow," she yelled over her shoulder as she rode up the street.

By the time Corey got home, she was sticky and sweaty, and so were the handlebars and seat of her bike. She shoved her bike into the garage, burst into the air-conditioned house, and slammed the door behind her. Yofi jumped up and licked the sweat off her arms.

"Is that you, kiddo?" called her father.

"Yes," gasped Corey. She stumbled into the kitchen.

"You're not going to let a little heat get you down, are you?" he asked. "Ready for that baseball game?"

"I guess so," Corey answered unconvincingly.

"You kids are so spoiled by air-conditioning these days. You need to get out and enjoy the summer. When I was your age, we didn't even have air-conditioning, just a few fans. And we didn't complain."

"I'm not complaining," said Corey. She ran her wrists under the cold tap at the kitchen sink and splashed water on her face.

They packed a Thermos of iced tea, threw bathing suits and towels in a bag, and put on their orange, black, and white Orioles baseball caps.

At the front door the heat blasted them. "You didn't tell me it was this hot!" her dad exclaimed.

They opened the doors and windows of the car to cool it off, but inside it still felt like a pre-heated oven. Her father fumbled with the keys and cleared his throat several times. Then, as if the thought had suddenly occurred to him, he said, "I've got a great idea! Let's skip the game and just go to the pool!"

Corey gave him a sly grin. "I've got an even better idea. Let's go jogging at the track, and then maybe we can play some tennis on those new asphalt courts."

Her father groaned. "Okay, okay, I admit it. I'm a wimp." He raised his eyebrows pitifully. "Can we please go to the pool now?"

"Oh, all right," she said, "if you insist."

Chapter 5

Only three and a half weeks into summer vacation and already Corey was bored. David was still at his dad's house in Annapolis, and Alex never answered the phone.

Corey's father was acting differently, too. He wasn't drinking, but he was getting awfully crabby, especially in the evenings. Often he snapped at Corey, and later apologized, saying it must be his nerves—shot from working in the heat all day.

Some days she went to the shop with her mother. She had become an expert at helping people find the perfect souvenir for Aunt Mabel or Uncle Martin.

The first heat wave had come and gone, followed by a week of muggy rain. Then one morning Corey woke up to find the sun shining and the birds singing. She got dressed and clomped downstairs in her flipflops, opened the front door and took a deep breath. The second heat wave had arrived.

Both her parents were busy getting ready to go to work, and Corey was tired of selling souvenirs, so she decided to give Alex another try. She didn't even bother to phone, but pulled out her bike to make the two-mile trek.

Alex and Laura were huddled on the front porch again, playing Barbies this time. Laura slurped an orange popsicle, which dripped orange syrup onto the Barbie clothes.

"Hi," said Corey as she pulled up.

"Corey, Corey, Corey," sang Laura.

Alex yanked a tuxedo jacket onto a Ken doll.

"Alex, you want to go to the mall with me?" asked Corey. She sat down and Laura scooted up close and wiped her orange mouth on the sleeve of Corey's T-shirt.

"I can't go," said Alex.

"Why not?"

"My dad's at work, and I have to take care of things here."

"Like what?"

"Like I have to watch Laura, for one thing."

Laura was back at the Barbie clothes, trying to fit a bikini top onto Ken. "How about if we take her with us?" asked Corey. "She won't be too much trouble."

"Come on, Corey. I need to stay home."

"Hey, Laura," asked Corey, "you want to come to the mall with me and Alex? It's air-conditioned, and we can buy ice cream cones."

"Oh, boy! Let's go right now." Laura jumped up and stomped around the porch. "We're gonna go to the mall," she chanted.

"Thanks a lot, Corey," said Alex.

"That's what I like about you, Alex," said Corey. "You're so agreeable."

Alex and Laura went inside to get some money, and Corey pulled a Kleenex out of her pocket and tried to wipe the popsicle syrup off her shirt. "Did your mom say you could go?" she asked when they returned.

"I didn't tell her," Alex said under her breath, so Laura couldn't hear. "We'll be back before she notices we're gone." They put Corey's bike in the garage and walked to the bus stop.

The worst part about the bus ride was, in a word: Laura. On the bus people either read or looked out the window or talked quietly, but Laura said everything that was on her mind, and with enough volume so that the whole bus could hear her.

"I lost a tooth yesterday," she announced.

"That's great," said Corey softly. "Shhh."

"It came out while I was eating dinner!"

"Laura, be quiet," began Alex.

"I spit it out, and there was blood all over my mashed potatoes."

Alex put her hand over Laura's mouth. "Shut up!" she whispered.

Laura looked out the window for about ten seconds.

"I've got boobs," she declared loudly.

Corey and Alex stared at her in shocked silence.

"They're not as big as my Barbie's, they're just little because I'm little. But they're still boobs."

Two boys in the seat in front of them jabbed each other and snickered. Corey hid her face. Alex grabbed Laura by the hand and marched her to the front of the bus. Corey followed.

31

"Could you please let us off here?" Alex asked the bus driver.

"Why are we getting out?" Laura whined as they went down the steps. "Where's the mall?"

"Great idea, Corey," Alex shouted as the bus roared away. "Sure, Laura won't be any trouble at all."

Corey looked at her sheepishly. "Sorry. But we can still walk to the mall. It's not much farther."

They trudged through the heat with trucks and cars spewing exhaust at them.

"Allie, I'm tired," said Laura in a high, thin voice that made her sound even younger than five and a half.

Alex sighed and picked her up.

Just once, thought Corey as they walked along, just once I'd like things to be normal. She imagined Alex's mother dressed in a skirt and blouse, driving them to the mall. She'd smile as she dropped them off at the entrance, and then take Laura with her to do some shopping. She'd say, "I'll pick you girls up at three o'clock, okay?" and they'd be free to roam the stores until then. That's how other people's mothers did it.

Finally, they reached the mall and pushed through the heavy doors into the cool, comfortable world of shopping. The first stop was for ice cream cones, which they ate in the "jungle," as Laura called it—benches set next to spraying fountains and tropical plants. Corey thought how strange it was that shopping malls made their insides look like outdoor parks. It was as if they didn't want to admit to being shopping malls at all.

"Have you ever had Italian ices?" asked Corey.

"You mean like Minestrone Chip or Lasagne Swirl?" asked Alex.

"No, silly." Corey laughed. "I mean real Italian ices. We got some when we visited Little Italy in New York last summer—"

Before she could finish, Alex nudged her with her elbow. "Speaking of Italian ices, look who's here," she said. Corey followed Alex's gaze and almost choked on her ice cream. There, across the palms and flowing fountains, sat Victor Donatelli.

"Who's that sitting with him?" Corey asked, trying to sound nonchalant. She didn't know Victor had a girl friend.

"Oh, geez, gag me with a fork. That's Marcia Demsey. She makes me sick," said Alex.

Marcia leaned toward Victor, her slender legs crossed gracefully, her long hair falling in a curtain against his shoulder. Corey couldn't wait to hear something awful about her. "Why does she make you sick?" she asked greedily.

"Gawd, her father is the pharmacist at the Giant, and her mother is on the PTA and is always dressed up and smiling and Marcia is so sweet to everyone, and the whole thing just makes me want to barf."

Corey stared at her friend in disbelief. "She sounds like a regular, normal kid," she said.

Alex's eyes flashed with anger. "Yeah, I know. I hate regular, normal kids. I mean, there are kids whose mothers get up and make them breakfast, and remind

33

them when it's time to go to bed, and help them with their homework and—and how about their fathers, Corey? They have fathers who keep their jobs and don't get fired every few months, and—"

"Stop it, Alex." Corey glared at her.

Alex stared past the potted palms at the happy couple on the bench. "Look at them," she said. "They have normal families and normal lives. You don't have to hate them. But you'll never be like them."

Her words cut through Corey like a knife.

"What has your dad been up to these days?" Alex asked abruptly.

"He's still working at the landscaping job."

"You know what I mean. What's he been *up* to?" She emphasized the word *up* as if it held special meaning.

Corey looked at her friend. "He's still not drinking," she said firmly.

"Great." Alex's voice was full of resentment. "Maybe I was wrong. Maybe soon you will be like Victor and Marcia."

"Alex, you know we're still in this together," Corey protested.

Alex rolled her eyes in disgust. "Yeah, right." She snatched a napkin off Laura's lap and roughly cleaned her sister's face.

Hot tears welled up in Corey's eyes and she turned away. Why couldn't Alex just be happy for her?

Finally, Alex sighed, giving up the fight. "Hey, listen, I need to get home before my dad comes back from work."

Corey sniffed.

Alex sighed again. "Come on, Corey, stop being so sensitive. Help me figure out a way to smuggle Laura home on the bus."

Corey wiped the tears from her cheeks. "Maybe we should buy a transistor radio and play it real loud so nobody can hear what she's saying," she suggested.

"Either that, or we can go buy a scarf and gag her."

Corey smiled. "Good idea."

They bought Laura a magic pen coloring book, and she was quiet the whole way home.

Chapter 6

Corey awoke with a start in the darkness of her bedroom. A familiar chill swept over her as the muffled voices took on words.

"Steven, you promised . . . ." Her mother was sobbing.

"Give me a break." Her father's voice, sluggish and thick, penetrated the wall between her parents' bedroom and her own. "Can't a man go out and have a good time with the boys every once in a while? I work pretty damn hard, you know."

Corey wrapped her pillow around her head and held it tightly against her ears. She remembered the evening before.

"Daddy probably just lost track of the time," her mother had said. "I suppose it's good for him to be out with friends. He's been so tense lately."

But Corey had seen the worried look in her mother's eyes. And four hours was an awful lot of time to lose track of.

The voices in the other room grew louder and angrier until her father stomped heavily down the hall, and the door to the guest room slammed shut. Then everything was quiet.

Corey shivered in the darkness. Her digital clock

blinked at her: 4:05. Outside, the crickets and cicadas sang as if nothing had happened. She stared out her window until the sky turned pink with early morning light. Over and over again she told herself the one piece of good news: "At least now Alex won't be mad at me."

Next thing she knew her mother was shaking her awake. "Time to get up, sleepyhead," she said. She sounded harried and as if she were trying hard to be patient.

"Why can't I stay asleep?" Corey groaned.

"Because your father is sick, and I need to go open the shop."

Corey groaned again and pulled the blankets over her head. After last night, she felt as if she could sleep all day.

"Corey, I need your help!" Her mother jerked the covers away. "I've made coffee, and I want you to give some to dad when he wakes up. And make sure he eats something. Oh dear! I almost forgot to call his boss."

Her mother rushed out of the room and down the steps to the telephone. Corey listened to the usual explanation: "Yes, I think it must be the flu . . . . I'm so sorry, I know you were counting on him. I'm sure he'll be up and around in a day or so . . . okay, I'll let him know. Thank you, Mr. Fitzgerald."

Corey slid her legs over the side of the bed and sat up. She rubbed the sleep out of her eyes and tried to look perkier than she felt.

Her mother ran back upstairs and listed a million

37

things Corey should do and another million things she should not do. Corey nodded yes so many times that she felt like one of those wooden puppets with a bobbing head.

After her mother finally left, the house was quiet. Corey tiptoed down to the kitchen. The longer her father slept, the more peaceful it would be. She sat on the floor with Yofi, and the hefty dog tried to crawl into her lap.

"Yofi, you're almost as big as I am, you silly thing. Here, you be my pillow." She picked up the comics section of the newspaper and lay down with her head on Yofi's side. The dog let out a happy, smothered sigh.

Before long Corey heard noises from upstairs: coughing and snorting, then footsteps to the bathroom.

She cringed as her father started down the steps. She hated those uncertain moments of not knowing what kind of mood he would be in.

He came around the corner. "Corey, don't lie on the floor like that! You'll trip someone and they'll break their neck."

Corey scrambled up off the floor. "Mom made some coffee. I can heat it for you," she offered.

Her father slumped down in a chair. His hair and clothes were rumpled, and he had dark rings under his eyes. Corey brought him the coffee and set it down in front of him. He smelled sour, like stale beer.

"Do you want anything for breakfast?" she asked timidly. "I can make eggs or something." He looked as though the thought of eggs nearly made him throw up and shook his head.

For several hours her father stared, zombie-like, at the TV and drank coffee. Among the million things Corey was supposed to not do were "don't run off with your friends" and "don't leave your father all alone." So she, too, sat and watched TV and soon felt as groggy as her father looked.

By mid-afternoon Corey decided that if she saw one more soap opera she would go crazy, so she got up to make lunch. She fixed peanut butter sandwiches, talked her father into eating one, and mentally checked off her list, "make sure your father eats something." She thought about Alex at home, taking care of her mother and doing her mother's job of watching Laura. And here she was, taking care of her father. Alex was right. They would never be normal kids like Victor and Marcia.

Her mother arrived home at dinner time with a sack of groceries and carry-out Chinese food in a big brown paper bag with grease leaking through the bottom. It smelled wonderful, like hot, steamy rice and spicy sauces. Corey set the table, but soon she saw that there would be no cheerful family dinner.

Her mother shoved a plate of Chinese food in front of her father while he watched TV. Then she stomped into the kitchen and slammed cabinet doors as she put away the groceries. Corey served herself some chicken chow mein and quietly went up to her room to eat.

Chapter 7

Corey had never liked roller coaster rides very much. But her life was quickly becoming just such a ride. Some days were calm, like the part of the ride where you clank along the flat section of track and nothing much is happening. Her father would go to work and have a few beers in the evening while everyone watched TV. Her mother would hum while she washed the dishes, and Corey would curl up with Yofi on the floor while she read a new book from the library.

And some days were like the part of the ride where the roller coaster car inches slowly up the steep hill, and your stomach tenses because you know what's coming next. Corey's father would drink more each evening, and sometimes he'd get mean and yell about stupid things like whether or not the TV channels were working right. Her mother's face would become strained, as if she were holding in so much anger that if she let it out, it would blow up the whole house. Corey tried to be as good as she could, but still they both found reasons to yell at her.

Then came the top of the roller coaster ride — that moment when the car seems to stand still, the moment when Corey could fool herself into thinking that everything was all right, that there was really nothing so strange about how her parents were acting. It only lasted a moment, though, before the roller coaster car came careening down, with everyone screaming and yelling, and Corey found herself hiding under her pillow in the dark.

After a night like that, her father would usually miss a day of work. Her mother would call Mr. Fitzgerald and tell him that her husband had a stomach virus or a bad cold or something. Corey hated to hear her mother lie like that. And she knew it was only a matter of time before Mr. Fitzgerald got tired of the excuses, and her father would be out of a job again.

With summer vacation almost over, Corey began to worry about starting junior high. She didn't much like the idea of changing classes seven times a day. Elementary school was bad enough with one teacher giving homework and detention. Multiply that by seven and you get junior high.

The school would be much bigger, too. How would she fit in with the hundreds of "normal" kids? In sixth grade, Alex's classroom had been right down the hall, and they'd seen each other at recess and lunch. What if they didn't have any classes together and got different lunch periods as well? Maybe she'd at least see David. After all, he wasn't too disgustingly normal, with his parents divorced and him always being shuttled back and forth between their houses.

A week before school started, David began living with his mom again. When Corey hung up after talking to him on the phone, her father asked, "Is that that little boy friend of yours?"

"Daddy, he's not my boy friend!"

"You know what I mean. He's a boy and he's your friend. Didn't you say he's a big baseball fan?"

"Yeah, he collects the cards and everything."

"Why don't you invite him to come with us to that Orioles game we never made it to this summer? We can get tickets for this afternoon."

Corey looked her father over carefully. Lately he'd been only drinking in the evenings and getting to work on time most days. He looked sober enough right now, anyway.

"Well, maybe—" she began.

"Come on, gal. Call him back. Let's have one more day of fun before you get locked up in that dungeon of a junior high school."

They made plans to pick David up, but Corey felt a nervous place in the pit of her stomach. Her father was sober now, but what if he didn't stay that way? She tried not to think about it.

At David's house, Corey's father waited in the car while she rang the doorbell. When David opened the door, she almost didn't recognize him.

Corey's mouth hung open. "David, you look so— different," she gasped.

"I do? What do you mean?"

"Well, you're so much taller, and—and your hair is shorter."

"Yeah, well, you're shorter and your hair is taller."

Corey laughed. She began to relax. How could anything go wrong with good old David around?

In the car, the three of them talked baseball most of the way to Baltimore, where the Orioles were to play the Yankees. Corey's dad had collected baseball cards when he was a kid, too, and since David knew all the current card prices, he was able to say just how much money Mr. O'Dell lost when his mother threw his cards away twenty years ago.

"You mean that Mickey Mantle card of mine would be worth two thousand dollars now?" Corey's father asked.

"Yep. And if you'd had his rookie card, and kept it in mint condition, you'd be able to sell it for a cool twenty-seven thousand."

Mr. O'Dell shook his head. "It's a crime what they let mothers get away with."

They pulled into the stadium lot and joined the jam of cars competing for parking spaces. Then they stood with hundreds of people to get tickets and afterwards waited in a long line to buy hot dogs and drinks.

"Isn't this great?" said Mr. O'Dell enthusiastically.

They found seats in the shade, cheered for the Orioles, ate three hot dogs apiece, and drank enough Coke to fill a small bathtub. The Orioles moved ahead with a home run in the bottom of the ninth inning and won the game, 8 to 6.

When the game ended, it appeared that everyone else in the stadium had drunk a lot of Coke, too, because the lines to the rest rooms stretched halfway around the stadium. Corey didn't want to be too obvious about her desperation to use the bathroom. She didn't want to embarrass David by talking about such things, so she asked politely, "Daddy, do you think maybe we could stop at a restaurant instead of waiting in these lines?"

"Yeah, Mr. O'Dell," said David, his face pained, his legs crossed as if he were about to pee in his pants, "I gotta go real bad!"

"Sure, let's go," said her father. "I know a place right nearby."

It took quite a while to exit the crowded parking lot, but once they were out on the road, Corey's father turned left and pulled up in front of a small, dumpy-looking restaurant. "Matt's Bar and Grill" read the peeling sign out front. They stepped out of the bright sunlight into the smoky pub.

"Why, if it isn't Steven O'Dell!" came a friendly voice from behind the bar. "I haven't seen you in ages, my man. And who are those munchkins with you? Would they be comin' in for a beer or two as well?"

As Corey's eyes adjusted to the dim light, she saw a short, chubby man in an apron, drying shot glasses with a white towel.

"Hey, Matt," said her father. "This is my daughter, Corey, and her friend David." David had begun to hop from one foot to the other. "Go on, you two. No sense standing here to be polite and then make a mess of the floor!"

Corey and David ran for the rest rooms. Through

the thin walls, Corey heard her father talking and laughing with Matt. When she came out, she found him at the bar with an empty beer glass. Matt slid another beer onto the counter. "Here you go. One for the road, eh?"

Her father put up his hand and shook his head. "Come on, now," Matt urged. "It's on the house, for my old friend Steven O'Dell."

Corey's father chugged the beer down the way most people chug water on a hot day. The nervous place in Corey's stomach knotted up again. But two beers wasn't much, she thought, just enough to make her father relaxed.

When they stepped outside, blinding sunshine surprised them. "Whoa, who turned on the lights?" Mr. O'Dell laughed.

Back in the car, they switched on the radio and cruised down the street toward the stadium and home.

"Oh, no! What's this?" Corey's father groaned as the traffic stopped dead.

"Must be an accident or something," said David.

"Either that, or just a million people all trying to get back to Washington at the same time."

They rolled down the windows, cranked the radio up full blast, and beat out the rhythms of the music with their hands on the dashboard and seats. Corey liked it when her father was lively like this.

"What did we do with those Orioles banners we bought?" her father asked.

Corey gave him a curious glance. "You put them in

the trunk, Daddy. Don't you remember?"

"Oh, yeah. Well, I'm going to check, just to make sure we've got them."

He put on the emergency brake and got out. Corey turned to look through the back window. She saw her father pull a brown bottle out of the trunk.

"I hope this traffic moves one of these days," she said quickly to David.

"Yeah. Hey, is your dad always this much fun?"

Corey laughed nervously. "Well, uh—sometimes, yeah."

Her father stepped back into the car. The sweet smell of whiskey hung around him and his eyes looked glazed. Corey took a deep breath and tried to calm the panic that rose inside her.

The line of cars began to creep forward until they passed a tow truck and a car with a crumpled bumper, and the traffic jam was over. Corey's father almost drove past their entrance onto the interstate and had to swerve like a race car driver to avoid missing it.

"Wow! You're a hot driver, Mr. O'Dell!" David exclaimed.

Corey gripped the door handle and clenched her teeth. She wanted the ride home to be over before they had an accident and before her father made a fool of himself in front of David. On the interstate, she watched the road and the other cars, ready to warn her father of the unexpected.

Soon they were pulling up in front of David's house. Corey breathed a huge sigh of relief.

"Okay, my boy," said her dad. "Let's get your banner out of the trunk."

"Thanks, Mr. O'Dell. I had a terrific time. I'll call you tomorrow, Corey."

Corey watched to make sure David entered the house. Her father brought his bottle into the car and took a few more swigs from it. Still, Corey relaxed. The most important thing to her was that her father hadn't done anything too strange in front of David.

As they drove home, she rested her head against the back of the seat. It had been a good day after all. She felt the cool breeze from the open window brush against her skin as she began to drift off to sleep. In her imagination, she could still hear the roar of the crowd cheering the Orioles to victory.

The sound of shattering glass yanked her awake. Corey heard shouting. She braced herself, expecting to feel the impact of a collision.

Nothing happened. The car was motionless under her. She opened her eyes and blinked in the glare of the setting sun. It was her mother who was shouting.

"Are you crazy—driving and drinking?! I'll break every one of your stupid bottles! You could have killed her!"

And her father yelling back, his words slurred, "Leave me alone, woman. I know how to drive a car!"

The car was parked in front of their house. On the sidewalk lay the shattered brown glass of her father's bottle, the liquor forming a dark pool on the cement.

As soon as Corey's mother saw that she was awake,

she whisked her out of the car and into the house. "Corey, you seem awfully sleepy," she said quickly. "Do you want supper, or do you just want to go to bed?" With her hand on Corey's shoulder she guided her toward the steps rather than the kitchen. It was quite obvious to Corey that her mother wanted her out of the way for the fighting. Didn't it ever occur to them that she could hear everything through the closed doors?

"I'll go to bed," Corey said as her stomach growled.

In her room, she turned her radio up loud to drown out their words. But she still heard shreds of the argument. She could have sworn she heard her mother say, "If you don't do something about your drinking, I'm going to leave you."

Chapter 8

During junior high orientation day, Corey and Alex were happy to find they had two classes together: gym, which was right after lunch, and English, seventh period right before they left to go home. They also found out that David had their same lunch period.

On orientation day, navigating her way through the halls seemed so simple. Corey located all of her classrooms, the gym, the cafeteria, the girls' room, and her locker. No problem.

The first day of school was not so easy. Two thousand kids all ran in different directions, each about to be late for the next class. When Corey tried to get to her locker, the flow of traffic carried her right past it, and she had to fight her way back. While she watched for room numbers, trying to find her math class, someone almost knocked her over. She felt sure that if she had fallen, she would have been trampled to death within seconds.

By the time Corey made it to the cafeteria for lunch, she was exhausted. She and Alex met at their appointed place, next to the à la carte line. They purchased their food and found seats near the windows.

"My social studies teacher stinks," said Alex.

"I don't like mine much either," said Corey.

"I mean literally. He stinks."

"You're kidding!"

"Nope. And have you seen the band teacher?"

Corey chimed in. "Yes! I couldn't believe it! Long curly hair down past his shoulders. He looks like a rock star. It made me wish I played an instrument."

"Me, too," said Alex. "Look, there's David."

David came over to their table and set down his tray.

"Hi, girls, how's it going? You been trampled by any ninth graders yet?"

They both nodded.

"David, did you see—" Corey began.

"The band teacher? Yep. And did you see Nicolette LeDoux? She grew over the summer!" The expression on David's face left little doubt as to what part of Nicolette had grown.

"Gross. You're not going to start with this puberty stuff, are you, David?" asked Alex in disgust.

David nodded enthusiastically.

"Hey, Liederman," a boy called. "Are you going to eat with us or flirt with girls the whole lunch period?"

David picked up his tray and winked. "Gotta go," he said.

"I hope David doesn't turn into too much of a brat now that his hormones are working overtime," said Alex.

Corey didn't answer. She stared dreamy-eyed across the cafeteria. Alex followed her gaze, but as soon as she saw who had caught Corey's attention, she shook her head.

"You've got to hang it up, girl. He's two years older than you, he doesn't even know you exist, and—"

"And I'll never be like him, right?" Corey finished her sentence for her.

"Right."

"Well, I can dream, can't I?" Suddenly Corey's face went slack. "Oh, no, Alex. He saw me looking at him. He's coming over! What am I going to do?" Corey grabbed Alex's arm.

Alex shook Corey's hand free. "Calm down, you idiot. Just act natural."

Victor looked taller and handsomer than ever.

"Hi, Corey," he said. "How's your first day of school going?" He leaned toward them, and Corey got a whiff of his after-shave.

"Okay," was all she could say. Alex kicked her under the table. "Oh, uh, this is my friend, Alex. Alex, this is Victor."

Alex and Victor smiled at each other politely.

"Well, if you have any questions, just let me know. I remember how scary it was to be a seventh grader."

Corey nodded and Victor left in search of lunch.

"Doesn't know I exist, huh?" she taunted Alex.

Alex was never one to lose an argument. "Is your dad still working the landscaping job?" she asked. It was more of a challenge than a question.

Corey looked down at her sandwich and tightened her lips. "No," she said softly. "He got fired."

"Oh," said Alex, "just wondering." She didn't need to say any more. Her point had been driven home.

Corey was silent.

"Listen, Corey," said Alex. "I'm not trying to be mean or anything. I just don't want you to be disappointed. Do you really want Victor to come pick you up for a date and see your dad passed out on the floor in his underwear?"

Corey shook her head. She remembered the day of the baseball game when her father was half drunk with David in the car, and how scared she'd been that he'd do something crazy. Then her mind went to the fight after the game and her mother's angry words about leaving.

"Alex?" she began.

"Hmmm?"

"Does your dad ever talk about leaving your mom, you know, because of her drinking?" The end of Corey's sentence faded to a whisper.

"Yeah. What a joke. Every time they have a fight, which is every other day, he says he's going to leave if things don't get better. And they don't get better, and he doesn't leave." She shrugged. "I stopped worrying about that a long time ago."

Corey let out a shaky sigh. "That's good," she said.

The bell rang, signaling the end of lunch and time for gym class.

"I just love to do jumping jacks and sit-ups right after lunch, don't you?" said Alex as they walked toward the gym.

Corey didn't answer. She watched the students rush by her in the crowded hallway, wishing more than anything that she could be like them — with their regular families and their normal lives. She hated the secret that made her different from all of them. And she was afraid she'd never find a place where she belonged.

Chapter 9

After a couple of weeks, school actually got better. Corey learned how to dodge people in the halls, and a few of her teachers even made class interesting. Victor waved when he saw her, and she and Alex enjoyed playing tennis in gym.

School got better, but home got worse. Her father still hadn't found a new job, and he was almost always drunk by the time she arrived home from school. Sometimes he was angry and mean and yelled at Corey no matter how hard she tried to be good. And sometimes Corey found him passed out on the couch in his underwear, just like Alex said. More and more she just tried to stay out of his way.

In gym class one day, the teacher handed out a sign-up sheet for after-school activities. Alex was late getting dressed for gym, as usual, so Corey grabbed an extra form for her. "Tennis, gymnastics, chess club," Corey read. "Participants may ride the activity bus home. It leaves school at 4:30 P.M."

"Late again, Williams," the gym teacher chided when Alex arrived. Corey handed her the form. "Let's sign up," she said.

Alex glanced at the paper and shook her head. Corey checked off one activity for each day of the week. The late bus would drop her off at around 4:45, and that only left about an hour alone with her father before her mother got home from the shop.

"What did you sign up for?" Corey asked Alex back in the locker room after class.

"Nothing," Alex answered dully.

"Why not?" Corey was disappointed.

"I don't like to leave Laura—I mean, my mom needs me to help her." Alex glanced sideways at the other girls changing clothes near them. No one seemed to be listening, but Corey didn't ask any more questions.

Alex slowly unlaced one sneaker at a time. Before she'd even taken off her socks, the rest of the class was dressed and combing their hair in front of the mirrors.

"Hurry up, Alex. I'm going to be late for my next class if I wait for you," said Corey.

"Don't bother," said Alex.

Corey sat down on the bench and crossed her legs. She could stay a few more minutes if it meant being a loyal friend.

After all the other girls had left, Alex finally took off her shorts and T-shirt. Not wanting to stare, Corey looked down at the books in her lap, but when Alex turned to reach into her locker, Corey glanced up. She wished she hadn't. Across Alex's back lay two wide red welts.

Corey gasped. "Alex, what in the world happened to you?"

Alex swung around. "What do you think happened?" she shot back.

Corey shuddered involuntarily.

"What's the big deal?" said Alex. "Doesn't your dad ever hit you when he's drunk?"

Corey shook her head. She felt like crying. "I didn't know your mom ever did that," she said softly.

"She didn't used to," said Alex. She jerked her clothes on and ran her fingers roughly through her hair. "Come on, let's go," she said.

Questions flooded Corey's mind. Does it still hurt? What did your father say? Does she hit Laura, too? Do you hate her? Are you going to run away? But one question bothered her more than all the others. She tried to ignore it, but it haunted her: If my dad keeps getting worse, is he going to do that to me?

Afternoon classes seemed to drag on forever. Corey tried to listen to her teachers, but her mind kept wandering.

In English class, she sent a note to Alex: "Do you want to do something this afternoon?"

Alex wrote back: "I have to go straight home."

That was no big surprise. Alex often seemed tense during English, watching the clock until three-thirty. Corey used to think Alex was bored. Now she knew the reason. She was worried about Laura, who got home at three o'clock from elementary school.

Corey wrote back: "I know. Can I come over and we'll hang out at your house?"

The answer: "No."

One thing about Alex, she was predictable. Corey wondered why she was writing these notes in the first place, when she could have answered them herself. She scribbled one more: "Fine. I'll walk you home."

At that moment, Mrs. Feinder, the teacher, came by with a ditto sheet on the proper usage of articles and predicates. It was just as well; Corey could have answered that last note, too. The answer would have been: "I can walk myself home."

At 3:21 Alex sat staring at the clock, nervously tapping her pencil on her desk. At 3:26 she packed up her papers and notebooks, and at 3:29 she got ready to bolt out the door when the bell rang. Unfortunately, Mrs. Feinder did not approve. She stopped Alex at the door.

"Alex, you seem very distracted. I noticed you quit working well before class was over." She sounded more annoyed than concerned.

"I—uh—I just wanted to be ready to leave on time." Alex squirmed.

"And what's so important that you have to spend the last ten minutes of class staring at the clock?"

"Nothing. Nothing is so important. I promise I'll work straight through from now on." She tried to scoot out the door, but Mrs. Feinder stopped her again.

"Alex, is there something wrong? Are you having a problem?" This time she actually sounded concerned.

"No, no. Nothing is wrong. I just promised my mother that I'd be home on time today so I could help her with some things." Alex flashed an innocent smile.

Corey wondered how she could lie so convincingly.

"Oh, isn't that nice," said Mrs. Feinder, relieved she didn't have to hear about any problems. "I guess you'd better go then." She waved the girls out the door.

Alex was livid. "Do you believe her? Making me stand there and babble about class when I have to get home!"

Corey trotted to keep up. "Maybe you should have told her," she said.

"Told who? Told who what? When?"

"Maybe you should have told Mrs. Feinder about your problem. I mean, she asked if you were having a problem."

A siren screamed past on a nearby street.

"I'm not having a problem. I can take care of Laura just fine if Mrs. Feinder would let me out of class on time." Around the corner from her house, Alex suddenly stopped in mid-stride and stared at Corey.

"What are you doing?" Alex asked accusingly.

"I'm walking you home," Corey answered.

"I can walk myself home."

"Alex, it's not just Laura I'm worried about—"

They rounded the corner to her street. What Corey saw shocked her like a slap of cold water. Red lights flashed steadily on a parked ambulance. A crowd of people was gathered in Alex's front yard.

"Laura!" Alex wailed. She dropped her books and bolted toward the house.

Corey's heart pounded as she sprinted after her.

"Where's my sister?" Alex shouted. "I can take care

of her myself. Get out of here! This is my house!"

A woman in a blue uniform grasped Alex by the shoulders. "It's all right, honey. Your sister's over there with Mrs. Neuman. And we're taking good care of your mom. Okay?"

Laura peered fearfully from behind a middle-aged woman. "Alex, come over here with me, dear," called the woman.

Alex ran to Laura and knelt down. "Are you sure you're okay?" she asked, inspecting her arms and legs.

Laura wrapped her arms around Alex's neck and wiped her nose on Alex's shoulder. "Mommy's not dead." She whimpered, her eyes wide with tears. "She's just sleeping."

Corey watched as two men wheeled a stretcher out of the house. Alex's mother lay on it with her eyes closed, her mouth open. "Mommy!" Laura began to sob. "I want to talk to Mommy!" Mrs. Neuman picked her up and held her close.

"Your mother had a bad fall, Alex," said Mrs. Neuman. "Laura found her at the bottom of the steps when she got home from school, and it scared her half to death. It's a good thing your sister cries loudly. I heard her all the way from next door."

Alex stared coldly as they slid her mother into the ambulance and closed the doors. "Does my father know?" she asked.

"They called him at work," said Mrs. Neuman. "He'll meet them at the hospital, and you and Laura are going to stay at my house until he gets home."

Alex turned to go with Mrs. Neuman as the ambulance siren started up. She waved once. "Bye, Corey," she mumbled.

As the siren's sound faded into the distance the other neighbors left and Corey began her long walk home. She decided not to sign up for any after-school activities.

At home she unlocked the door and stepped inside. Yofi yawned, stretched, and came to nuzzle her.

"Shhh," she whispered and patted him on the head.

In the den, her father lay sleeping on the couch. Corey covered him with the green and red afghan. Then she opened a can of beef stew and dumped it in a pan. If he woke up, she'd heat it and try to get him to eat.

Her heart raced as she opened the kitchen cabinets and drawers, searching through them, moving pots and cans and dishes as quietly as she could.

Then, thinking, she stood still for a minute. Yofi came and sat on her foot. Next she searched the bathrooms, each cabinet, closet and drawer. The toilet in one bathroom was running. She jiggled the handle.

Aha! she thought, the workshop in the basement. She moved cans of paint and jars of spackle, looking through the shelves and under the counters. Nothing.

Back upstairs, the toilet was still running. She lifted the heavy porcelain tank cover and placed it on the floor. When she turned to look inside the tank, she went pale. There it was.

She'd planned to pour all the liquor she found down

the sink, to get rid of it forever. She'd put an end to all this craziness. But suddenly she felt weak, afraid of what he might do to her when he found it missing. She put the tank cover back on with shaking hands.

In the den her father still slept. His unshaven face made him look old and haggard. For a second Corey saw not a sleeping man on a couch but an unconscious man on a stretcher. She took a sharp breath. "You've got to stop, Daddy," she said aloud.

This time she moved with determination. She opened the toilet tank again and dipped her hand into the cold water to retrieve the bottle. She emptied the contents into the sink and buried the bottle deep in the kitchen trash. There were whiskey bottles in the other two toilet tanks as well, and the next to go was one she found under the mattress in the guest room.

Then she sat down in the overstuffed armchair in the den and waited for her father to wake up.

Chapter 10

Saturday morning Corey lay sprawled across her bed, her chin propped up on her arms, watching cartoons on the portable TV. Her father hadn't said a word about the missing bottles. He'd also started a new job—one his brother Bob got for him at his office.

In the middle of a commercial with dancing ten-year-olds dressed up like rock stars, Corey's mother came to her door.

"Corey, I need to talk with you," she said, her mouth set in angry lines.

Was her mother going to yell at her for dumping the bottles?

"Hurry and get dressed. I'm leaving for—uh—the shop in a half hour. I want you to come with me."

Corey got dressed and brushed her hair. If she were going to the shop, no matter how much trouble she was in, she wanted to look nice in case Victor came by. She fixed her bangs with the curling iron and enough hair spray to keep them in place for a week. She put on blue eye shadow, tried to cover her freckles with some foundation, and brushed on a touch of blush.

"Hi, Victor, how've you been?" she said to the mirror and flipped her hair smartly behind her shoulders.

Nope. Not quite right.

"Hey, Victor. Watcha been up to?" She put one hand on her hip and gave the mirror a coy smile.

That was even worse.

She was about to try a third variation when a loud voice yanked her back to reality.

"Corey! I'm leaving right now!"

She grabbed her jacket and raced down the steps.

"I'm ready, Mom."

Corey and her mother drove in silence, until Corey noticed where they were. "Mom, you took a wrong turn!" she exclaimed.

"No, I didn't," said her mother firmly. "We're not going to the shop."

Corey stared at her. "Where *are* we going?"

"I got a phone call this morning," she said, "from a woman at Uncle Bob's office."

Oh, no! thought Corey, Daddy's lost another job after only working for two weeks.

Her mother gripped the steering wheel and cleared her throat. "She's a social worker. She said she wants to talk to me—to us, if you'll come with me."

Corey's stomach felt as though there were live fish flip-flopping inside. A social worker. Social workers were for poor people and homeless people, or divorced families where one parent tries to take the kids away from the other. Why would a social worker want to talk to them?

"She said we could come see her today," said her mother, "while the office is empty."

Corey nodded, though she didn't know exactly what she was agreeing to. She hadn't been to her Uncle Bob's office since she was in third grade, but she remembered the high ceilings and winding staircase of the Victorian mansion that housed his contracting business.

The office was quiet. They walked down the hall to a room that had Employee Assistance Program stenciled on the door. A tall woman in a navy blue suit greeted them.

"Hi! Nancy O'Dell? I'm Ellen Conrad. And this must be Corey."

Corey flinched. The social worker already knew her name. What else did she know?

Corey's mother shook Ms. Conrad's hand, forcing a smile, then looked around the room for a place to sit. To Corey she looked more like she wanted to find a way to escape.

Ms. Conrad invited them to sit in two leather armchairs in the corner near her desk. "I know this was a difficult decision for you, Nancy. I'm glad you came."

Corey's mother fiddled with her purse strap and looked down at the floor. "My husband is not a bad person," she said. "He's been under a lot of stress lately, and he drinks to relax—"

"I know," said Ms. Conrad.

"It's just that his drinking has gotten worse, and —I don't know what to do."

"I know," said Ms. Conrad again.

It was strange for Corey to hear her mother talk

about her father's drinking. At home they never said a word about it.

"I'm so sorry it has been affecting his work. I just need to know what to do to make him stop."

"I know," said Ms. Conrad for the third time. "I've heard your story a thousand times, and I have some good news and some bad news. The bad news is, I can't help you find a way to make your husband stop drinking. No one can."

"Then why did you call me to come down here?" Corey's mother demanded.

Ms. Conrad continued, her voice calm. "Because there is a way to help your husband decide for himself to get help. We have a very effective alcoholism intervention program here."

"How dare you call my husband an alcoholic!" Corey's mother slammed her palm down on Ms. Conrad's desk. "He has some problems with stress and some problems with his work habits, but he is *not* an alcoholic!" She grabbed her purse and stood up to leave.

Corey stood up, too, alarmed. The word "alcoholic" hit her like a punch in the stomach. Alcoholics were drunks who wore dirty clothes and slept in the street and begged for money. Her dad was definitely not a drunk.

Ms. Conrad pulled a pamphlet from her drawer. "Before you walk out, Nancy, why don't you look over this questionaire. See how many items you answer yes to," she said.

Corey's mother took the pamphlet and eyed it as if it might bite her. Corey moved beside her and they read together:

Is Someone You Love an Alcoholic?
1. Has he/she lost time from work due to drinking?
2. Is drinking making your home life unhappy?
3. Does he/she drink to escape worries or trouble?
4. Has he/she ever had a "blackout" or temporary amnesia after a drinking episode?

The list went on. As they read, Corey's mother wrote her answers in the margin. Her hand shook as she held the pencil.

"I only answered yes to half of them," she said when she'd finished. "Only eight out of sixteen."

Ms. Conrad took the pamphlet and read from the next page. "If you answered yes to any one of the questions," she read, "that's a warning sign that your loved one might be alcoholic, and if you answered yes to any two, there's a very good chance that your loved one is an alcoholic." Ms. Conrad looked up at Corey's mother and hesitated. "It says that if you answered yes to three or more, there is little doubt that your loved one is an alcoholic."

Corey's mother sank back in her chair and pressed her fingers against her forehead. Corey squirmed and wished she were at home watching cartoons.

"Nancy, I want you to understand that alcoholism is not just a nasty habit or a sign of moral weakness. It's a physical disease."

Mrs. O'Dell blinked back tears. "Then there isn't any hope? You mean there's nothing I can do?"

"It's as I said before," Ms. Conrad told her gently. "There is nothing you can do to make him stop drinking. He needs to decide for himself. But there is something we can do together to help him decide to get help. Would you like me to tell you about it?"

"Yes, please," Corey's mother answered.

After that, Corey heard a lot of big words like "intervention" and "rehabilitation facility" and "hospitalization insurance," and other things she didn't understand at all like "hitting bottom" and "bringing the bottom up to the alcoholic." She watched a pigeon strut back and forth on the windowsill and then fly off into the grey autumn sky.

Finally her mother stood up and shook Ms. Conrad's hand.

"This is not a decision you can expect to make right away," said Ms. Conrad. "Why don't you think about it for a few days?"

"I will." Corey's mother blew her nose. "It's just all so new. I hadn't realized he was sick."

Corey took her mother's hand and squeezed it. She didn't want her father to be sick, and she didn't want her mother to be upset, and she felt confused and scared herself.

"Just remember, Nancy," said Ms. Conrad. "Interventions don't work every time, but they do work in three out of four cases. If you decide to go through with it, we'll hope for the best."

Chapter 11

Alex hummed as she split open her bag lunch. "Mrs. Neuman makes great sandwiches. Oh, boy! Turkey!"

Corey inspected the square of shriveled-up pizza on the tray in front of her. It looked like something she should be learning about in biology rather than something she should be eating.

"All right!" Alex continued. "Homemade cookies for dessert. Hey, Corey, Mrs. Neuman is taking me and Laura roller-skating after school. Want to come?"

Corey jabbed at the pizza with her fork. "Nah," she answered.

"What's wrong with you? You always used to want to do stuff after school," said Alex, her mouth full of turkey sandwich.

Corey sighed. "Something weird is going on at my house."

"Like what weird?"

"Promise you won't tell anybody?" asked Corey.

"Who would I tell?"

"Anybody!"

"Okay, I won't."

Corey leaned toward Alex. "I think my mom might be planning on—"

"Hi, guys!" It was David. "Hey, Alex. How's your mom doing?"

"She's okay. The doctors said she'll be in the hospital for a while longer. In the meantime, I'm enjoying Mrs. Neuman's cooking."

"Mrs. who?"

"Mrs. Neuman, our next-door neighbor. My dad is paying her to take care of me and Laura while my mom is in the hospital."

"David," Corey asked suddenly, "how did you decide whether to live with your mom or your dad?"

"I didn't decide. My mom got custody. What made you ask?"

"I was just wondering," said Corey. "I mean, if the child was older, like say almost thirteen, do you think they would let the child decide who to live with?"

"I don't know," said David. He pushed his tray toward Corey and slid into the chair next to her. "Corey, is there something you're not telling us?"

"No," she answered. She felt herself blush. "I mean, yes. But I'm still not telling you."

"Are your parents splitting up?" he asked.

Corey's lips started to quiver. David put his arm around her shoulders. "Come on, Cor. It's not so bad. I've learned to live with it."

"Is *that* what I wasn't supposed to tell anybody?" asked Alex.

"Yeah," Corey answered reluctantly.

"Did you tell somebody?" David asked Alex.

"How could I have told anybody when I didn't even know yet?"

"Why did she ask you not to tell anybody when you didn't know anything to tell?"

"Because she didn't want anyone to know."

"Then why did she tell me?"

"She didn't tell you, Dufus Brain," said Alex. "You guessed."

David raised his eyebrows. "Oh-oh. I'm sorry, Corey. But I won't tell anybody, I promise."

"Me, too," said Alex.

"I don't know that they're splitting up. I just—" began Corey.

"Then why did you tell us they were?" interrupted David.

"I didn't tell you, remember?" said Corey. She was beginning to feel like a defendant on the People's Court. "I just think maybe my mom is planning on leaving my dad." There, she'd said it.

There was an uncomfortable silence. Finally Corey said, "Listen, I'll just let you guys know when I find out what's going on. Okay?"

Alex and David both sighed with relief. "Sure, that's great," said David.

"Good deal," said Alex.

That evening, Corey's mother was too tired to make dinner, so as usual Corey fixed a can of soup for herself.

As she did her homework in the living room, she heard her mother talking on the phone. Her voice sounded worried. Corey followed the extra-long phone cord from the kitchen into the dining room, through the foyer, and saw where it disappeared into the front hall closet. From behind the closet door she heard,

"I'm glad I decided to go through with it. Tomorrow, yes. Thanks so much for all your help, Ellen."

Corey felt the strength drain out of her as if she'd sprung a leak. Her mom was talking to Ellen Conrad, the social worker. She wanted to shout, "Mom, don't leave him! He'll get better!"

In bed, Corey lay awake for a long time. Sometime during the night, she heard the guest room door slam and knew that her father had come home.

The next morning Corey's alarm clock jarred her from sleep. She dressed in jeans and a sweatshirt and started toward the bathroom. In front of her parents' bedroom door Corey stopped as she heard drawers open and close, and her mother's footsteps cross and recross the room. She lifted a fist to knock just as the door swung open.

"I didn't know you were there, Corey," her mother said, startled and guilty-looking. She pulled the door closed behind her, but not before Corey had seen the packed suitcase lying open on the bed.

Corey dashed to the bathroom. She turned on the water in the bathtub, sat down on the edge of the tub, and began to cry. She stayed there until it was time to go to school and her mother shouted upstairs, "Corey, you're going to be late!"

Corey patted her swollen eyes with a cold, wet washcloth. She walked slowly down the steps.

"Bye," she called.

"Don't you want breakfast?" her mother called from the kitchen over the banging of plates as she emptied the dishwasher.

"I'm not hungry," Corey answered.

Suddenly, she knew she couldn't leave the house. "Bye, mom," she called again, louder this time. Then she opened and shut the door as if she'd just left and slipped into the front hall closet. She closed the closet and sat down on the pile of boots.

The soft wool coats around her smelled like her family, her home. Corey grabbed the end of her father's coat and laid her cheek against it. She curled up and soon dozed off.

The phone's harsh ring pulled Corey from sleep. At first she thought it was her alarm clock, and she didn't understand why she was in the closet on a lumpy pile of coats and boots. Then she remembered.

"Yes, Bob, we'll wait for you." Corey heard her mother tell Uncle Bob. "Steven's not up yet anyway. See you in a little while then."

The doorbell rang. Her mother's footsteps sounded in the hall.

"Hello, Ellen." It must be Ellen Conrad. "I'm really glad you got here early. I'm so tense I could scream."

"That's to be expected." Corey heard Ms. Conrad reply.

Corey stretched her cramped shoulders. The doorbell rang again.

"Moira! How good to see you," said Corey's mother. "It's been so long. How was your flight?"

Moira? Corey's Aunt Moira had flown in from Connecticut? The doorbell rang a third time. Was her mother planning a divorce or a party?

"Mr. Walters, please come in. Here, let me take your coat. This is Steven's sister, Moira O'Dell, and—" She opened the closet door to hang up Mr. Walters' coat. Corey blinked in the sudden light. "And, uh—this is my daughter, Corey." She reached for Corey's hand and helped her up. Corey smoothed her hair and smiled weakly at Mr. Walters. She'd never met him before, but knew he was her father's boss at his new job.

Mr. Walters laughed. "That looks like a nice place for a nap," he said.

Mrs. O'Dell hung up his coat and then pushed Corey ahead of her into the dining room.

"What in the world are you doing?" Her mother was frantic.

The tears came easily again. "I was so scared. I thought you were leaving Daddy—"

Ms. Conrad stood in the doorway watching. Mrs. O'Dell looked at her helplessly. "Why don't you let me talk to her?" said Ms. Conrad. "You've got enough to worry about. Steven just got up."

Corey's mother rushed from the room. The doorbell rang again, and Corey heard her Uncle Bob call, "Hello? Can I come in?"

"What's going on around here?" Her father's angry

voice boomed from upstairs. "Every time I try to fall back asleep, the stupid doorbell rings."

"Corey," said Ms. Conrad hurriedly, "we're doing an intervention with your father. We thought you were too young to be here, but now that you are, I think you can really help."

Corey crossed her arms over her chest. "What's an intervention?" she demanded, alarmed that these people would plan something for her father without her.

"We're going to see if we can get your dad to go for treatment for his alcoholism. Everyone here has written down the ways his drinking has affected them, and they've practiced it with me, kind of like a script. And now they're going to tell these things to your father and ask him to get help."

Corey frowned at Ms. Conrad. She had no right to barge into her family like this!

"Corey, this may be your father's only hope to get well. I'm really sorry we didn't include you sooner— your mother was afraid it would upset you. But now I see we've upset you by *not* telling you. Can you forgive us, and can you help?"

Corey bit her bottom lip. "All right," she said.

Ms. Conrad took Corey's hand in hers. "I want you to tell your father how his drinking has affected you. Describe some times when his drinking made you feel angry or sad or hurt. And tell him that you love him and you want him to get help. Do you think you can do that?"

74

Corey tensed inside. She'd never talked to her father about his drinking before. But if it might give him a chance to get well, she would try.

"Okay," she answered.

"Good. It sounds like everyone is ready. Let's go."

In the living room, Corey ran to her Aunt Moira and buried herself in her hug.

"Corey, I thought you'd be in school," said Aunt Moira.

Corey shook her head. "I'm going to stay here."

Uncle Bob led Corey's father in and sat him down on the couch. His clothes were rumpled, and his eyes puffy and red. He looked anxiously around the room. When he saw Aunt Moira, he jumped up.

"What's going on? Did somebody die? Is it Mother?" he cried.

"Mother is fine, Steven," said Aunt Moira. "You're the one we're worried about."

"Let's get started," said Ms. Conrad, as everyone took a seat. "Nancy, I believe you're first."

Corey saw her mother's hands shake as she unfolded a sheet of notebook paper. "Steven, I've asked these people to help because I don't know what to do anymore." She glanced at Corey's father. He stared at the floor. She took a deep breath and read from the paper. "When you drink, your whole personality changes. You get nasty. Last month we were leaving a party and I wanted to drive because you were very drunk. You got so angry at me that in front of everyone you shook me and threatened to hit me. I was horribly embarrassed.

But the worst was the ride home with you driving. I thought you would kill us both."

Mrs. O'Dell's voice trembled. She looked imploringly at Corey's father, who refused to meet her eyes. Ms. Conrad nodded for her to continue.

"Each night when you're out, I jump when the phone rings. I think it's the police calling to tell me you've been in an accident. I'm scared, Steven. I want you to get better. I love you, and I want you to get help." Corey wanted to shake her father, to make him look up and pay attention.

Ms. Conrad nodded at Aunt Moira.

"Steven," Aunt Moira began, "I always looked up to you as my big brother, and I always loved spending Christmas with you and your family. But the past few years have been awful. Last year you were so drunk during Christmas dinner you knocked over a bowl of gravy and then blamed it on Nancy for putting it in front of you. And by the time we were ready to open presents, you were sitting all alone at the kitchen table with a bottle of scotch talking to yourself. I felt as if we were kids again, the way Daddy used to get drunk on holidays and make a scene.

"I don't want you to end up like Daddy, Steven. If he'd stopped drinking when the doctors told him to, he would probably still be alive today. I love you, Steven. Please get help."

Corey watched her father tap one foot nervously.

It was Uncle Bob's turn next. "Steve, when I got you this new job at my office, I didn't realize how bad your

76

drinking was. I remembered what a hard worker you used to be, but over the past few weeks you've been late almost every day. Last week at our lunch meeting with a new client you drank heavily and then started telling dirty jokes. I had to apologize a dozen times to the client just to keep him from taking his business elsewhere.

"You've got lots of potential, Steve, but you're drowning it in alcohol. Dad had a disease, and he died from it. He passed that disease on to us—to you and me. It was a hard day when I finally turned and faced the truth—that I'm an alcoholic. But if I hadn't admitted it and quit drinking, I'd be dead by now."

Uncle Bob leaned forward. "It's time for you to face the facts, Steve. You're an alcoholic. And you're the only one who can do what needs to be done to get well. I love you, Steve. I'm asking you to get treatment."

Corey wasn't sure what "treatment" meant, and the word seemed to jar her father as well. He glanced up for a moment and she tried to catch his eye.

Mr. Walters was the next to speak. "You're a good man, Steve. On your clear days, your work is topnotch. But too often you're drunk on the job or you leave work early after a five-martini lunch. If you go for treatment for your alcoholism, I'll support your efforts and your job will be waiting for you when you come back. If you refuse treatment, you're fired."

Corey's father wrung his hands and shifted uneasily in his seat. "What do you mean, 'treatment'? What's all this about 'when I get back'?" he demanded.

"You have a decision to make, Mr. O'Dell," said Ms. Conrad. "There's a bed waiting for you at an alcoholism treatment center, and your wife has packed your suitcase."

"I'm working on it," said Corey's father. "I can quit. I quit last summer. I don't need treatment, for God's sake. If it will make you all happy, I'll quit. Okay?"

Corey wanted to wrap her arms around him, he looked so scared.

"There's one person who hasn't spoken yet, Mr. O'Dell," said Ms. Conrad. "I suggest you listen to your daughter before you make your decision."

Corey twisted the corner of her sweatshirt and tried to remember what she was supposed to say. Her father lifted his eyes to meet hers.

"Daddy," she began, "remember my birthday when you promised we'd go for a hike along the canal with Mom and Yofi? But then my birthday came, and you just stayed in bed all day. And last year when I was in the school play you said you'd come see me, but you never came home from work that day." Corey heard her own voice waver and hoped she could keep going. "Last summer when you quit drinking we did lots of fun stuff together—"

Corey stopped. Her father was staring at her, his eyes wild like those of a trapped animal. Beads of perspiration stood out on his forehead. "And I love you, Daddy. Please get well."

"You have a disease, Mr. O'Dell," said Ms. Conrad. "The disease of alcoholism doesn't just go away. For

78

your own sake, and for the sake of your family, I suggest you go for treatment."

Corey's father stood up and pulled out his handkerchief to wipe his face. He looked at Corey, then at his wife, his expression seeming to plead for this whole thing to end. Then he turned and walked out of the room and out of the house.

"What now?!" Corey's mother gasped, turning to Ms. Conrad.

"Now all we can do is pray," she answered.

A heavy silence filled the room. Corey's mother and Aunt Moira sniffled and Uncle Bob coughed and cleared his throat. Ms. Conrad sat and fidgeted with her pen.

Corey normally divided prayers into three categories, small, medium, and big, measured by how much she wanted what she was praying for and how hard she figured it would be for God to give it to her. She tried not to ask for too many really big things each year, because she didn't want to be selfish with God's time. The prayer she prayed this morning, she decided, was big enough so that she wouldn't ask for another thing until next summer. It was simple: "Please let Daddy say 'yes'."

The sound of the front door opening startled everyone. Corey ran to find her father standing in the doorway, his shoulders slumped, his head down. She took his hand and walked with him into the living room.

"It's not fair," he mumbled. He ran one hand through his hair and shook his head. "Wasn't it Dad who always used to tell us 'Life isn't fair'?" His eyes shifted from one person to another.

Suddenly he threw his hands up and let out an anguished groan. "Okay, you win. I'll go."

Corey's mother jumped up and threw her arms around his neck. Everyone cried and laughed and hugged each other.

Finally Corey's dad pulled away and sank into an armchair. Corey climbed onto his lap the way she used to when she was in the first grade.

"Thank you, Daddy," she said in his ear.

He hugged her hard, as though he didn't want to let go.

Chapter 12

The house felt empty with her father gone. It seemed strange that he never pulled his car into the driveway, never showed up tired and hungry for dinner, never slammed a door coming in late at night. Corey looked forward to Sunday, her first family visiting day at the treatment center, with a mixture of excitement and dread. What would the place look like? Would the other alcoholics stare at her the way they did on the streets in Washington? Would her dad be angry that everyone made him go to that place?

Sunday morning there was no time for dawdling in bed. Her mother had made it clear that she must be ready to leave for the treatment center on time. If they were even one minute late to the family education program, the doors would be locked and they wouldn't be allowed to see her father at all. Corey thought it sounded like jail.

"Are there bars on the windows?" she asked in the car.

"On what windows?" her mother asked.

"At the treatment center."

"Of course not!" her mother sputtered. "It's not a prison, Corey. It's a rehabilitation center—kind of like a hospital."

The image in Corey's mind of a dreary, run-down building with black bars on the windows and armed guards out front shifted to that of a metal and glass high-rise with sanitary hallways and doctors and nurses rushing around. But when they arrived, neither image proved accurate. The building was long and low, of clean white brick. Enormous picture windows faced a wide lawn with beds of yellow chrysanthemums.

Inside, they passed an exercise room filled with weight machines and a TV lounge with two comfortable couches. Corey decided it looked like a cross between a health club and a hotel.

Corey gripped her mother's hand as they entered a large room set up with rows of folding metal chairs and a movie screen.

"Let's sit in the back." Corey tugged on her mother.

"I won't be able to see the movie," she said and guided Corey to seats in the front row.

Corey squirmed in her seat, crossing her legs first one way and then another. "How long till we get to see Daddy?" she asked.

"Shhh. As soon as this is over," her mother answered.

Corey watched the other people out of the corner of her eye, trying not to appear too curious. There were a couple of kids her age and lots of noisy smaller kids. Most of the adults in the room were women.

At eleven o'clock on the dot, a tall, handsome man in a three-piece suit walked to the front of the room. He must be one of the doctors, thought Corey.

"Hi, my name is Mel," he said as the room quieted down. "I'm an alcoholic and a drug addict. I'm one of the counselors here at the center, and I'll be glad to answer any questions you have after the movie."

The movie was about a family where the father was an alcoholic and the mother and children did everything they could to keep his life running smoothly even though he was often drunk. They kept him out of trouble with his boss and bailed him out of jail when he got caught drunk driving. And they tried to make him stop drinking, but nothing worked. Then, toward the end of the movie, they stopped taking care of things for him, and the father got very sick, and a doctor got him to go to a treatment center.

"Why did they stop taking care of him?" Corey asked her mom afterwards. "That was mean."

"Why don't you ask Mel?" Her mother nudged her.

Corey nudged her right back. "I don't want to. You ask him."

"It's your question."

Corey looked up and saw to her horror that Mel was watching her. He grinned.

"Did I hear a question, young lady?"

Corey's biggest question at the moment was, Why did we have to sit in the front row? But she managed to squeeze out the words, "Uh—I was wondering why the mother and kids in the movie just let the dad get worse. Why didn't they help him like they did at the beginning?"

"Did you used to take care of your father sometimes?"

Mel asked. "Fix food for him, make sure he ate it, watch him so he didn't take a drink?"

"Yeah," said Corey.

"Well, one of the things we try to teach you here is to stop doing so much for your father. Did you ever think it was strange that you were just a kid and you were taking care of a grown-up?"

Corey nodded.

"I'm speaking to all of you." Mel raised his voice. "Before they came in for treatment, I'll bet your alcoholics and drug addicts acted like children sometimes. They expected you to call in sick for them when they were hung over, pay the bills when they were out of work, and clean up after them when they broke things or threw up."

People agreed, murmuring "That's right."

"And you did all of those things," Mel went on, "and you felt like you were helping them."

He walked up and down the aisle, looking directly at people as he spoke. "But instead of helping, you were making things worse. You were keeping them from seeing how much trouble alcohol was causing in their lives." Mel pointed a finger at his subdued audience. "When they come home, you need to treat them like adults. And adults don't need children to take care of them."

He walked toward Corey and put his hand on her shoulder. "You've all got your own lives to live. Let your addicted family members live their own lives

84

again, too. That's what *your* part of recovery is all about."

When there were no more questions, Mel dismissed them and they filed into the halls. Corey caught sight of her father in the TV lounge. She squealed "Dad!" and ran full speed into his arms. He swung her up and hugged her, then plopped her down, and gave her mom a long, gushy kiss. Corey looked away during the kiss. A boy a little older than she was sat on one of the couches watching TV. Next to him was an elegant-looking woman wearing a black silk pantsuit and diamond earrings.

"It is so good to see you both!" Her father was all smiles.

"How're you feeling?" Corey's mother asked him.

He held his hands out flat in front of him. They shook visibly, like the trembling hands of an old man. "If the D.T.s would leave me alone, I'd be a lot happier. The doc here says it'll get better every day."

Corey's mother grasped his hands. "I'm so sorry, honey. I wish we'd known how bad it was."

"How could you have known? I kept most of it hidden." He put his arm around her. "Let's go outside. There are benches and a little more privacy."

As they walked away, Corey turned to look at the boy and woman again. "Daddy, why aren't they—I mean, why don't they go find their—"

"You mean why didn't anyone come visit them today?"

"Visit *them?*"

"Their families are from out-of-town and won't be able to visit every week. They call on the phone, though."

Corey still hadn't gotten over the shock. "You mean they live here?"

"That's Randy. He fifteen, and he's in the teen program. He's an alcoholic and a drug addict. And Layla is an alcoholic like me. She's in my counseling group." Corey's father smiled at her surprise. "One thing I've learned about this disease is that it can strike anybody, no matter what their age, no matter how much money they have."

Outside they found a bench and sat together. Her father told them about his Alcoholics Anonymous meetings and classes where he learned about his disease, his counseling groups and exercise sessions. He was more talkative than he'd been in months. And there was something else different about him, too. As he talked, Corey studied his face, trying to figure out what had changed.

He talked about how it had taken him most of the week to realize how powerless he was over alcohol—how he really had lost control over his drinking. Then, suddenly, in the middle of one of his sentences, Corey realized what it was.

"Daddy!" she said excitedly. "You're getting fat!"

Instead of scolding her for interrupting, he laughed. "Hey, don't rub it in! The doc weighed us yesterday and I found out just how fat, too, but I'm not telling." He patted his stomach. "Lots of people here have gained weight. When we were drinking and drugging, we weren't eating, but now we eat three meals a day. I'm going to have to watch it if I don't want to be a real blimp when I come home."

When it came time to leave, Corey's father walked them to the car.

"Can't we stay just a little longer?" Corey asked.

"Honey, if I'm even one minute late getting back in that building, I won't be allowed to see you next week."

Corey stared at him. It was beginning to sound like jail again. But the strangest thing was that her father, who had always hated rules, seemed ready to do whatever these people told him.

"Don't you mind all the rules around here?" she asked. "Doesn't it make you feel like you're a little kid or something?"

Her father hesitated a moment. "No," he said, "actually it makes me feel as if I'm finally growing up."

He gave her one last hug, and her mother one last kiss, and then ran back to the building where Mel held the door open for the last few stragglers. Corey watched as he disappeared into the building and Mel closed the door behind him.

Chapter 13

Corey nibbled at her lunch. She kept looking around the cafeteria, watching each group of students as if she'd lost someone.

"Trying to find your lover-boy?" teased Alex.

"Nope. I was just thinking." She leaned closer to Alex. "We're not as different as we thought. Did you know that out of every six kids, one of them lives with an alcoholic parent?"

"How do you know?"

"My dad told me."

"Your dad spied on them?" Alex was not impressed.

"No, dummy, they told him about it at the rehab."

"You mean people from the rehab spied on them?"

"Alex, I'm talking statistics here. I don't know which ones are from alcoholic homes, I just know that some of them are. Lots of them. And I don't feel so different anymore, that's all."

Alex glanced around the cafeteria. "I think Bubba Brooks must be one of them. He's definitely weird."

"Alex, nobody said that these kids are weird. Do you think I'm weird? How about you? Do you think you're weird?"

Alex thought a minute. "Everybody's different, and I'm no different from anybody else," she said.

Corey rolled her eyes.

"My mom is coming home tomorrow," Alex changed the subject. She lifted the top piece of bread off her sandwich and rearranged the contents. "Laura is all excited."

"Aren't you excited?" Corey asked.

Alex shrugged. "In the hospital they kept her off the booze. But when she comes home, who knows?"

Corey cast her eyes down. The old guilt feelings poked at her.

Alex must have read her mind. "Listen," she said, "I hope your dad stays sober. Last time when he stopped drinking I was really jealous, and I just wanted us to be the same again. But now I know what it feels like not to worry about her every day—and I hope he makes it, that's all." Alex took a huge bite and looked away, embarrassed that she'd been so generous.

"I hope your mom makes it, too," said Corey.

Alex shrugged again. "Mmm-hmm," she said through a mouthful of tunafish.

"Are you going to David's birthday party?" asked Corey.

Alex swallowed. "Now there's a mystery for you," she said. "David comes from a perfectly normal divorced family, but he's the weirdest of all. How do you figure that?"

"I'm not the one deciding who is weird and who isn't. And what's so weird about David, anyhow?"

"He invites girls to his birthday parties."

"He invites you and me to his birthday parties."

"That's what I said. He invites girls to his birthday parties."

"Alex, you're the weird one."

"That's because I come from an alcoholic home." She smiled smugly.

Corey sighed in exasperation. "To answer your question, I'm not going to David's party because it's on Sunday, and that's the day I visit my dad." A smile crossed Corey's face and she waved timidly in the direction of the cafeteria door.

"Lover-boy," said Alex, without even turning around.

"Would you please stop calling him that?" said Corey. "Shhh! Here he comes."

Victor pulled up a seat. "Hi, girls! How's the cafeteria food today?"

"Same old slop. That's why I'm not eating it," said Alex. "Ruggelah." She pointed to the rolled up apricot-filled pastry she was eating for dessert.

"Looks good," said Victor. "Hey, Corey, what's happening with the shop? I've been going down to help my parents on Sundays, and your mom's place is always closed. She's not sick or anything, is she?"

"Uh—no. It's just the slow season," said Corey, pleased with her quick cover-up until she realized it was already November, and Christmas shopping time, which was certainly not the slow season. "But she'll be opening on Sundays again soon—for the Christmas rush and all."

"So I'll see you down there sometime?" said Victor.

"Sure," said Corey.

After he'd gone, Alex looked at Corey and cocked her head. "Weird," she announced.

"Victor is not weird," objected Corey.

"Not him. You." Alex sunk her teeth into the ruggelah.

The weeks passed quickly, and the days grew colder. Finally, Corey's father's thirty days at the rehab center were over and he came home. "I really want this to stick," he said at dinner that first night. "One of my friends from the rehab got out two weeks ago and already slipped up. I don't want that to happen to me."

After dinner each night, he grabbed his coat and rushed out the door to an Alcoholics Anonymous meeting. "Mel told us to go to ninety meetings in ninety days and then call him," he explained. "He said the support of other drunks will help keep me sober."

He left the house at 8:15 and got home at 9:45. Corey always waited up until she heard him come in. Then she fell asleep listening to her parents talk.

On Thursday evening her father left at 8:15. At 9:50 he still wasn't home, and Corey started worrying. At 10:00 her mother told her to turn out her light and go to sleep. At 10:45 Corey stomped into her mother's room.

"He's supposed to be home by now!" she nearly shouted.

Her mother looked up from the book she was reading. "Honey, it's not past your father's bedtime, but it *is* past yours."

"Aren't you going to do something? Call his friends, or call the—" She couldn't bring herself to say "bar."

The front door opened. Corey flew down the steps, then stood with crossed arms and scowled at her father.

"It's late. Where were you?" she demanded.

Her father blinked in the foyer light. "Corey, what are you doing up?"

"I was worried. You were supposed to be home at nine forty-five. Do you realize it's almost eleven o'clock?" She tried to sound strong, but her voice wavered.

"I thought the family education program was supposed to help her go back to being a kid again," Mr. O'Dell said to his wife, who had followed Corey down the stairs.

Corey's mother suppressed a smile. "I don't know. Sounds to me as if you're grounded for the rest of the weekend."

Corey stomped her feet. She couldn't stand them making fun of her. "I was worried!" she bawled.

Her father folded her into his arms and kissed the top of her head. "Were you afraid I was drinking again?" he asked.

Corey nodded and sniffled. Her father held her away and looked at her. "I want you to listen to me. You can't keep me sober. Only I can keep me sober."

"Will you promise me?" Corey pleaded. "Will you promise you won't ever drink again?"

He shook his head. "That's not the way it works, Corey. I can't promise anybody anything—not even myself. All I can do is keep on doing the best I can, one day at a time. And I can stay sober today."

"Where did you go tonight then?" she asked.

"A group of us from the A.A. meeting went out for pizza. Those people are getting to be my friends—because they understand. They know what it feels like to be an alcoholic."

The question was out of Corey's mouth before she could stop it, probably because she'd wondered for so long. "What does it feel like, Daddy?"

The three of them sat down on the foyer steps, and Yofi padded over and laid his head in Corey's lap.

"Before I started drinking, it felt like the whole world knew how to talk and crack jokes and have fun—everyone except me. I was too shy to dance or to make anyone laugh. I felt as if I were watching life from the outside, and no one had invited me to join in the fun. I just didn't feel as though I belonged."

"I've felt that way too," Corey wanted to say, but she didn't interrupt.

"Then I had my first drink. All of a sudden, I felt like the king of soul." He jumped up and danced a few steps. "I could dance like a pro, I could sweet-talk the girls." He grinned at Corey's mom. "And I could have fun. And the more I drank, the more fun I had. And the

93

more people liked me, because I was the wild one, the life of the party."

Corey's mother laughed and shook her head. "I remember those days!" she said.

Corey's father winked at her. Then he knelt in front of Corey and looked into her eyes. "But the booze turned against me," he said. "After a while it wasn't much fun anymore, and most of the time it just made me sick." He hung his head. "But by then I was addicted, so I kept on drinking. I couldn't stop."

He stood up and ruffled Corey's hair. "So, I'm starting over. I'm learning to have fun and laugh without a beer in my hand, and I went to my first sober party tonight. A pizza and Pepsi party at Pizza Hut, with a bunch of drunks."

"And did you have fun?" asked Corey's mother, smiling.

"Absolutely," he said. "We were so loud the manager had to come and tell us to quiet down."

"Really?" Corey asked, wide-eyed.

"Yep. We didn't dance, though. We figured they'd throw us out if we danced."

Corey pictured her father dancing on a tabletop at Pizza Hut. She giggled.

"Listen," he said. "It looks as if I weren't the only one who got sick from this disease. You two spent so much time taking care of me and worrying about me, you forgot what it was like to just live your own lives."

Corey's mom agreed.

"There's a place I'd like you to come with me tomor-

row night, where they have meetings for everyone—
A.A. for me, Alanon for you, Nancy," he said to Corey's
mom, "and Alateen for you, kiddo. I'll bet they've even
got Ala-dog for Yofi." He gave the dog a pat on the
head. "The meetings are supposed to help you focus
on yourself and your own problems instead of mine."

"It sounds good," said Corey's mother.

"Then, afterwards, everyone goes out together for
ice cream at Friendly's," he added.

"That sounds even better," said Corey. She yawned.
"Can we go to bed now?"

Corey's father put his arm around her and walked
her to her room. From the edge of her bed, he leaned
over to kiss her goodnight. She wanted to ask him,
"Daddy, do you feel as though you belong now?" but
she was too sleepy. She hugged him tight, then rolled
over, and fell asleep.

Chapter 14

"Because it sounds like fun, and anyway, my dad wants me to go," Corey stuffed her books into her locker and turned to face Alex.

"Corey, with your dad going straight, you finally have a chance to be a normal kid. I don't see why you want to go hang out with a bunch of weirdos."

"Alex, just answer me. Do you want to come with us or not?"

"No way. But let me know if you see Bubba Brooks there."

"I won't be able to tell you anything. It's an anonymous program, and you're not allowed to talk about it outside the meetings."

Alex took a few steps backwards down the hall. "So have fun at your secret meeting." She waved and left.

Corey pulled out her coat and shoved her locker shut. If Alex wouldn't come with her, she'd just have to brave the Alateen meeting alone. It would only last one hour, then she'd meet her parents and go out for ice cream.

The parking lot was already crowded with cars when the O'Dells pulled in. Small groups of people stood outside talking, some of them drinking coffee from white paper cups.

"Hey, Steve," a grey-haired man called to Corey's father. "Bring those pretty ladies over here and introduce me."

"Hi, Lou," said her father. "This is my wife, Nancy, and my daughter, Corey. This is their first meeting."

Lou shook her mother's hand. "I hope you folks like it here. If you don't, we'll gladly refund your misery."

Corey's mother laughed.

"Come on, Corey," said Lou. "I'll show you where Alateen meets." He led her to a room with a circle of chairs and several teenagers in it. Corey sat in a chair as far away from everyone else as she could and picked at her nails.

The meeting started with a welcome from Sandy, an energetic woman a little older than Corey's mom, wearing black stretch pants and a bright pink sweatshirt. "Is this a first Alateen meeting for anyone here tonight?" Sandy asked.

Corey swallowed hard and raised her hand timidly.

"Welcome," said the group in unison.

After that, Sandy asked who would like to talk. One girl told how her father came in drunk on Halloween, went to the closet instead of the bathroom, and peed in her bag of Halloween candy. "He's such a dweeb," she said in disgust. Then she shrugged. "I guess my H. P. decided I'd get zits if I ate all that chocolate." She looked toward the ceiling and laughed. "Thanks a heap, H. P.!"

"Can someone explain 'H. P.' for the newcomer?" Sandy asked.

A boy with shoulder-length hair and one silver earring raised his hand. "H. P. is your Higher Power," he said. "It's like whatever you want it to be, as long as it's not you. It can be God or, if you don't believe in God, it can be the group, like your Alateen or A.A. group." The boy looked at Corey as he spoke. She studied the floor tiles.

Mercifully, as soon as the H. P. explanation was over, another boy began to speak, "So my mom is drunk as a skunk, as usual, and she's all pissed off because I say, 'No, I don't have time to hose out the garbage cans because I've got to get to work on time.' And she says, 'You stupid idiot, I told you about this last week, blah blah blah.'" The boy scratched his head and continued, "You know, it used to be when she put me down, a voice in my head would agree with her. It would say, 'Yeah, stupid, why can't you do anything right? You're such an idiot.' But yesterday, she says, 'You stupid idiot,' and this voice says, 'She's wrong. She's sick. Don't believe her.' Just like that!" He grinned. "Hey, maybe I am getting better. This recovery stuff isn't too bad!"

Other kids nodded and agreed.

As Corey listened she kept wondering where she fit in. Did she belong with these kids, many of whose parents were still drinking? Or did she belong with the "normal" kids now that her father was sober? No one in the room looked particularly strange or weird, as Alex would say, except possibly the guy with the silver earring.

Several kids had walked in late, and when the door opened to let in one more latecomer, Corey looked up. She wasn't the least bit prepared for who she saw. Her hand flew over her mouth as she let out a tiny gasp. Victor gave her a surprised smile and sat down.

There must be some mistake, thought Corey. Victor must have been looking for a Sons of Italy reunion and walked into the wrong room. She had major trouble listening during the rest of the meeting.

At the end, Sandy made an announcement about an Alateen dance coming up and invited the group to join hands to close. "Keep coming back, it works," they recited together.

"What we do here, who you see here, what you hear here, let it stay here," Sandy added.

"Here, here!" called the rest of the group.

As the meeting broke up, Victor moved over next to Corey. "I guess you're as surprised to see me as I am to see you, huh?" he asked.

Corey nodded. "Yeah, really." She wanted to tell him he couldn't possibly be as surprised as she was, but she held her tongue.

"My dad and I are going out for ice cream at Friendly's with everyone. Do you want to come?" Victor asked.

"Sure. My parents were planning on it," Corey answered.

"Great! My dad is down at A.A. I'll go ask him if you can ride with us." And he was out the door.

Corey felt her cheeks flush hot pink. Victor Donatelli had just asked her out!

When she found her parents, they were talking to a group of men and women. Corey watched her father's eyes sparkle and his hands move as he talked. He looked as if he'd found a place to feel comfortable, a place where people liked him and thought he was lots of fun with no alcohol to make him "lively."

Victor came running down the hall, smiling. "My dad said yes. And we promise to have you home by midnight."

"I haven't asked my parents yet!" Corey pretended to object.

But she knew they'd say yes. And she knew she would sit at a table at Friendly's with her mother and father and Victor and his father. And she knew she would order one scoop of vanilla ice cream with butterscotch sauce and pecans on top. And she knew that finally she had found a place where she belonged.